CLASSIC
HORSE
& PONY
STORIES

A DORLING KINDERSLEY BOOK

Produced by Leapfrog Press Ltd
Senior Editor Naia Bray-Moffatt
Art Editors Miranda Kennedy
Adrienne Hutchinson
Picture Research Liz Moore
Additional Illustrations Rob McCaig
John Woodcock

For Dorling Kindersley
Senior Editor Alastair Dougall
Managing Art Editor Jacquie Gulliver
Production Erica Rosen

First published in Great Britain in 1999 by
Dorling Kindersley Limited, 9 Henrietta Street,
London WC2E 8PS
Visit us on the World Wide Web at
www.dk.com

Compilation copyright © 1999
Dorling Kindersley Limited
Illustrations copyright © 1999
Dorling Kindersley Limited

A CIP catalogue record for this book is available
from the British Library.

ISBN 07513–7433–4

Colour reproduction by Bright Arts in Hong Kong
Printed by L.E.G.O. in Italy

CLASSIC
HORSE
& PONY
STORIES

Selected by
DIANA PULLEIN-THOMPSON

Illustrated by
NEAL PUDDEPHATT

DORLING KINDERSLEY
London • New York • Delhi • Sydney
www.dk.com

CONTENTS

FOREWORD by Diana Pullein-Thompson

Wild and free, cherished and admired, trained and sickly, we meet horses in all kinds of situations in this anthology: Spanish ponies shipwrecked on their way to work in the gold mines of Peru; a wild Australian mare terrified that a man will capture her beloved foal. Flicka, a mustang on the point of death, nursed back to life by a boy; Black, a fiery stallion, heavily handicapped but still battling to win a race after a bad start.

Find out about horses in the New World on page 15

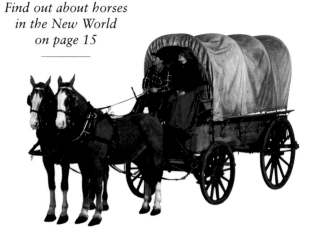

The story of how Black Beauty is broken in is told on pages 42–46

The breaking in of Patagonian Mancha by cowboys contrasts starkly with the gentle training of Black Beauty by his kind and thoughtful master. There are stories told by children, too: Briony, Lynne and David struggle to save Candy's colt – "if policemen can deliver babies, why can't they deliver a foal?" We jump in the gymkhana with unorthodox Jill, and join John and Tess in rescuing noble cart horses from the knacker's yard. Myth and humour have long been part of the horse world. So we read of Pegasus, the great winged horse, who carries a hero over dark mountains and deep seas until he finds and kills the deadly Chimera. We laugh with Lewis Carroll's Alice as she watches a ridiculous knight's hopeless attempts to ride a real horse when he would be better off with a wooden one on wheels.

I hope you will enjoy these very different and exciting stories. Most of all, I hope that when you put down the book you will have a greater understanding of the true nature of those most lovable of animals, the horse and the pony.

Fun exercises to improve riding technique are described on page 51

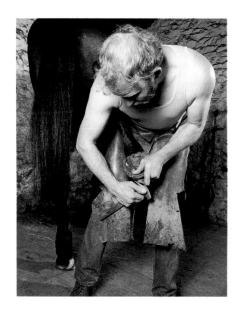

Basic horse care is discussed on page 81

Jill's exciting day at the gymkhana is described on pages 82–90

LIVE CARGO!

from *Misty of Chincoteague* by Marguerite Henry

The story of how horses arrived in North America – and ran wild.

A wild, ringing neigh shrilled up from the hold of the Spanish galleon. It was not the cry of an animal in hunger. It was a terrifying bugle. An alarm call.

The captain of the Santo Cristo strode the poop deck "Cursed be that stallion!" he muttered under his breath as he stamped forward and back, forward and back.

Suddenly he stopped short. The wind! It was dying with the sun. It was spilling out of the sails, causing them to quiver and shake. He could feel his flesh creep with the sails. Without wind he could not get to Panama. And if he did not get there, and get there soon, he was headed for trouble. The Moor ponies to be delivered to the Viceroy of Peru could not be kept alive much longer. Their hay had grown musty. The water casks were almost empty. And now this sudden calm, this heavy warning of a storm.

Cupping his hands to his mouth, he bellowed orders.

He plucked nervously at his rusty black beard, as if that would help him think. "We live in the latitude of white squalls," he said, a look of vexation on his face. "When the wind dies, it will strike with fury." His steps quickened. "We must shorten sail," he made up his mind.

Cupping his hands to his mouth, he bellowed orders: "Furl the topgallant sail! Furl the coursers and the main-topsail. Shorten the fore-topsail!"

The ship burst into action. From forward and aft all hands came running. They fell to work furiously, carrying out orders. Meanwhile, in the dark hold of the ship, a small

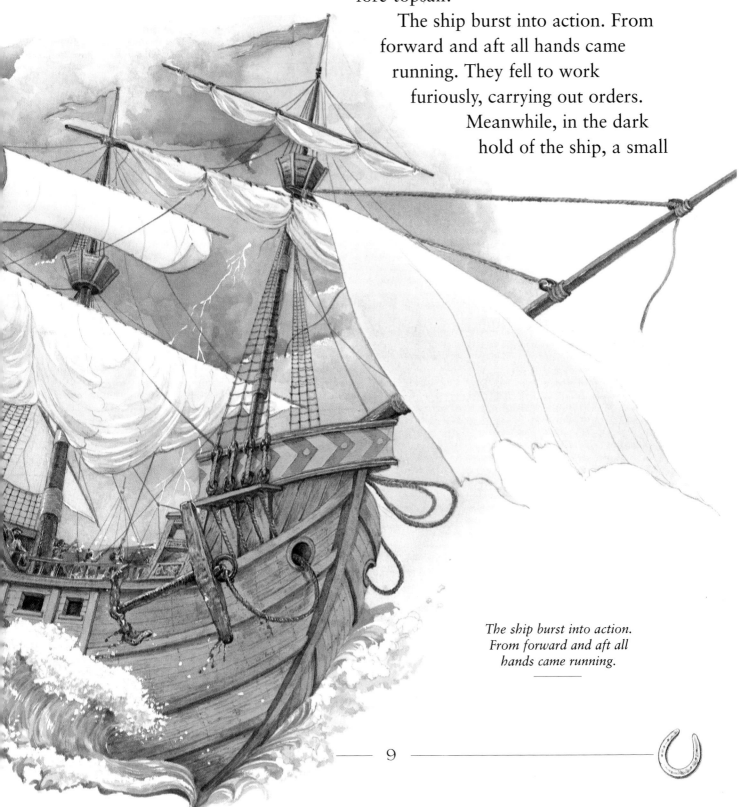

The ship burst into action. From forward and aft all hands came running.

bay stallion was pawing the floor of his stall. His iron shoes with their sharp rims and turned-down heels threw a shower of sparks, and he felt strong charges of electricity. His nostrils flared. The moisture in the air! The charges of electricity! These were storm warnings – things he knew. An inner urge told him that he must get his mares to high land before the storm broke. He tried to escape, charging against the chest board of his stall again and again. He threw his head back and bugled.

From stalls beside him and from stalls opposite him, nineteen heads with brown eyes whited. Nineteen young mares caught his anxiety. They, too, tried to escape, rearing and plunging, rearing and plunging.

But presently the animals were no longer hurling themselves. They were being hurled. The ship was pitching and tossing to the rising swell of the sea, flinging the ponies forward against their chest boards, backwards against the ship's sides.

A cold wind spiralled down the hatch. It whistled and screamed above the rough voice of the captain. It gave way only to the deep flump-flump of the thunder.

The sea became a wildcat now, and the galleon her prey. She stalked the ship and drove her off her course. She slapped at her, rolling her victim from side to side.

Suddenly the galleon shuddered. From bow to stern came an endless rasping sound. The ship had struck a shoal. And with a ripping and crashing of timber the hull cracked open. In that split second the captain, his men, and his live cargo were washed into the boiling foam.

The wildcat sea yawned. She swallowed the men. Only the captain and fifteen ponies managed to come up again. The captain bobbed alongside the stallion and made a wild grasp for his tail, but a giant wave swept him out of reach.

The stallion neighed encouragement to his mares who were struggling to keep afloat, fighting the wreckage and the sea. For long minutes they thrashed about helplessly, and just when their strength was nearly spent, the storm died as suddenly as it had risen.

The sea was no longer a wildcat. She became a kitten, fawning and lapping about the ponies' legs. Now their hooves touched land. They were able to stand! They were scrambling up the beach, up on Assateague Beach, that long, sandy island which shelters the tidewater country of Virginia and Maryland. They were far from the mines of Peru.

The ponies were exhausted, and their coats were heavy with water, but they were free, free, free! They raised their heads and snuffed the wind.

The smell was unlike that of the lowland moors of Spain, but it was good! They sucked in the sharp, sweet pungence of pine woods, and somewhere mixed in with the piney smell came the enticing scent of salt grass.

In that split second the captain, his men, and his live cargo were washed into the boiling foam.

*They seemed unable to believe that the
island was their own. Not a human
being anywhere. Only grass. And sea.
And sky. And the wind.*

The stallion's hunger stirred him into action. He rounded up his mares, and with only a watery moon to light the way, he drove them through the needle-carpeted woods. The mares stopped to eat the leaves of some myrtle bushes, but the stallion jostled them into line. Then he took the lead. Through bramble and thicket, through brackish pools of water, he led the way.

The moon was high overhead when the little band came out on grassy marshland. They stopped a moment to listen to the wide blades of grass whisper and squeak in the wind, to sniff the tickling smell of salt grass.

This was it! This was the exciting smell that had urged them on. With wild snorts of happiness they buried their noses in the long grass. They bit and tore great mouthfuls – frantically as if they were afraid it might not last. Oh, the salty goodness of it! Not bitter at all, but juicy-sweet with rain. It was different from any grass they knew. It billowed and shimmered like the sea. They couldn't get enough of it.

The ponies forgot the forty days and forty nights in the dark hold of the Spanish galleon. They forgot the musty hay. They forgot the smell of bilge water, of oil and fishy odours from the cooking galley.

When they could eat no more, they pawed shallow wells with their hooves for drinking water. Then they rolled in the wiry grass, letting out great whinnies of happiness. They seemed unable to believe that the island was their own. Not a human being anywhere. Only grass. And sea. And sky. And the wind.

At last they slept.

The seasons came and went, and the ponies adopted the New World as their own. They learned how to take care of themselves. When summer came, and with it the greenhead flies by day and the mosquitoes by night, they plunged into the sea up to their necks in the cool surf. The sea was their friend. Once it had set them free. Now it protected them from their fiercest enemies.

Winter came, and the grass yellowed and dried; but the ponies discovered that close to the roots it was still green and good to eat.

Even when a solid film of ice sealed the land, they did not go hungry. They broke through the ice with their hooves, or went off to the woods to eat the myrtle leaves that stayed green all winter.

Snow was a new experience, too. They blew at it, making little flurries of their own. They tasted it. It melted on their tongues. Snow was good to drink!

The stallion's hunger stirred him into action.

If the Spaniards could have seen their ponies now, they would have been startled at their changed appearance. No longer were their coats sleek. They were as thick and shaggy as the coat of any sheep dog. This was a good thing. On bitter days, when they stood close-huddled for comfort, each pony could enjoy the added warmth of his neighbour's coat as well as his own.

This was it! This was the exciting smell that had urged them on. With wild snorts of happiness they buried their noses in the long grass.

NEW WORLD HORSES

In the early 16th century, Europeans set sail to conquer the newly-discovered Americas, bringing horses with them. It is possible that some of these horses were shipwrecked, and survived to form herds in the wild. European arrivals were the first horses to live in the Americas since their ancestors died out there 10,000 years earlier. They soon bred, and there are 25 million horses living in the Americas today.

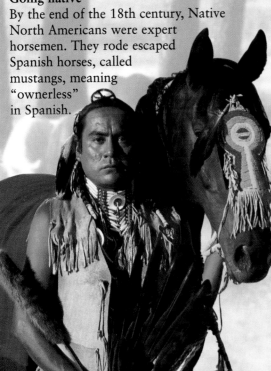

Cortez in Mexico
In 1518, Spaniard Hernando Cortez arrived to conquer Mexico with 5 mares, 11 stallions, and 600 soldiers. These tough horses trekked 42 km (26 miles) a day and terrified the natives, who had not seen horses before. Cortez said he conquered Mexico because of them.

Going native
By the end of the 18th century, Native North Americans were expert horsemen. They rode escaped Spanish horses, called mustangs, meaning "ownerless" in Spanish.

Go West
Horses became true American pioneers. In the mid-19th century, they pulled wagons full of white settlers 3,300 km (2,050 miles) from the east of the United States to the west.

Island life
The story describes how wild horses came to live on Chincoteague and Assateague islands, off Virginia. It is historically more likely that they were abandoned rather than shipwrecked. They were discovered in the 1920s and the publication of Marguerite Henry's book in 1947 made them famous. About 200 live on Assateague today.

Born in the Wild Wind

from *The Silver Brumby* by Elyne Mitchell

This extract from the first book in a hugely successful series captures Elyne Mitchell's wonderful insights into the behaviour of wild horses.

Once there was a dark, stormy night in spring, when, deep down in their holes, the wombats knew not to come out, when the possums stayed quiet in their hollow limbs, when the great flying phallangers that live in the mountain forests never stirred. On this night, Bel Bel, the cream brumby mare, gave birth to a colt foal, pale like herself, or paler, in that wild, black storm.

Bel Bel had chosen the birthplace of the foal wisely. He was on springy snowgrass under a great overhang of granite that sheltered them from the driving rain. There he lay, only a pale bundle in the black dark, while Bel Bel licked him clean and nuzzled him. The wind roared and howled through the granite tors above in the Ramshead range, where the snow still lay, but there was no single sound of animal or bird except the mournful howl of a dingo – once, twice, it rang out and its echo answered, weird and wild.

Bel Bel lifted her head at the sound, and her nostrils dilated. From the shadowy mass between her forefeet came a faint nickering cry and she nuzzled him again. She was very alone with her newborn foal, and far from her own herd, but that was how she had felt it must be. Perhaps because of her colour, so much more difficult to hide than bay, or brown, or black, or grey, or chestnut, she had always led a hunted life, and when a foal was going to be born she was very nervous and hid herself far away. Of the three foals she had had, this was the only one creamy, like herself.

*On this night, Bel Bel, the cream brumby mare, gave birth to
a colt foal, pale like herself, or paler, in that wild, black storm.*

Bel Bel felt a surge of pride, but the pride was followed by fear. Her
son would be hunted as she was and as her own cream mother had been
before her – hunted by man, since they were so strange looking in the
wild herds. And this colt would have another enemy too, every stallion
would be doubly against him because of his colour.

The wind roared and the rain was cold, so cold, as if it would turn to
snow. Even with the shelter of the rock, the storm was beating down on
them, the moving darkness was becoming a thing of terror. The howl of
the dingo came again. Bel Bel nosed the tiny colt to get up.

He heaved up his head, stuck his long forelegs out in front of him,
and gave a little snort of fear. Bel Bel pushed him up till he stood, his feet
far apart; long legs trembling; then she nosed him, wobbling, bending,
step by step to the sandy mouth of the cave, and there, just out of the
rain, she let him tumble down again.

Soon it would be time to make him drink, but for the moment, out of
the wild storm, he could rest. Dawn must come soon, and in this storm
there would be no men abroad to see a cream brumby mare lead her

Bel Bel nosed the tiny colt to get up. He heaved up his head, stuck his long forelegs out in front of him, and gave a little snort of fear.

newborn foal through the snowgums to where there would be grass for her to eat and longed-for water to drink. Bel Bel really knew that there would be very few men in the mountains till all the snow had gone and they were driving their herds of red and white cattle, but the fear of Man was never far from her thoughts.

Dawn came very slowly, showing first the dark outline of the cave mouth against a faintly lighter sky, then, on the hillside below them, reaching long fingers of forest right up to the rocks, the wind-tormented heads of snowgums, driven and lashing as though they must tear themselves up by the roots. The rain had stopped.

Great massive clouds kept racing up over the mountains but, as the light grew strong, the sky began to look as if it was being torn in shreds by the wind. Flying streamers of rain-washed blue sky appeared and Bel Bel, feeling very hungry herself, decided it was time the foal should drink and that the day would be fair enough for a newborn colt to go with his mother to some better pastures.

"I will call you Thowra," she said, waking him with her nose, "because that means wind. In wind were you born, and fleet as the wind you must be if you will live."

On that first day, while the storm blew itself out Bel Bel did not take Thowra far, only down through the snowgums to a long glade that led to a heather-banked creek where she could drink. That night they went back to the opening of the cave and the foal slept on the dry sand curled up against his mother's flank.

The next day she decided to take him farther, to a wide, open field in the snowgum forest, where the grass grew very sweetly, and where the creek ran shallow over a sand and mica bottom.

The storm had died in the night and there was warm spring sunshine. Bel Bel noticed with pride how the foal trotted more strongly by her side. She did not hurry him, often stopping to graze as they moved under the snowgums or in the long glades. She never left the shelter of the trees without first pausing and looking carefully into the open country ahead. Thus it was through a curtain of the leathery snowgum leaves that she looked out onto the wide sunny field, and saw a bay brumby grazing in the distance by the creek.

Bel Bel became completely still, watching, then she recognized the bay as a mare of her own herd, Mirri, who had been caught by a stockman as a yearling and managed to get free. Mirri, for this reason, was very nervous of men, and she and Bel Bel had often run together, away from the herd, when they thought the others were getting too close to the stockmen's huts.

Now Bel Bel made out a dark shape near Mirri and knew that the bay mare, too, had had her foal. Unafraid, she led Thowra out to join them.

She looked out onto the wide sunny field and saw a bay brumby grazing in the distance by the creek.

When Mirri saw them coming she gave a whinny of greeting, and Bel Bel arched her neck a little and stepped proudly beside her creamy son, thinking how his mane and tail were silver and would some day look like spray from a waterfall as he galloped.

Mirri was pleased to see her.

"Well met, Bel Bel," she said, "and what a fine foal you have – creamy too! I must stir my sleepy-head to show him off!" And she nosed the bright bay at her feet.

The bay raised his head sleepily, but, seeing strangers, he became wide awake and struggled to his feet.

"A fine intelligent head," Bel Bel said. "What do you call him?"

"Storm," Mirri answered. "He was born in the worst of the weather, two nights ago. And yours?"

"Thowra, for the wind. He was born then, too. They will be great mates for a year or so," and both mothers nodded wisely, for it was the way of the wild horses that the young colts should run together, after they left their dams, until they had reached the age and strength to fight for a mare or two of their own and start their own herd.

Storm and Thowra sniffed at each other curiously and then both turned back to their mothers for a drink.

Sunny spring days came, day after day, and the grass grew fresh, and green, and sweet. The two mares stayed in Snowgrass Plain, eating, basking in the sun, drinking the cold, clear water, growing strong and sleek after the hard winter, and giving their foals plenty of milk. The foals grew strong, too, and romped and galloped, and rolled in the sun.

Soon they learned to recognize the great wedge-tail eagles floating in the blue arch of sky above them, knew the call of kurrawongs, and were unafraid of the friendly grey kangaroos or little brown wallabies.

The two foals were equal in strength and size, and when they were able to follow their mothers for quite a distance, Bel Bel and Mirri, who had become restless to rejoin the herd, started moving off to the south.

For an hour or so they travelled across the ridge-tops in the fringe of the snowgums, and by mid-morning they came out on an immense open

Sunny spring days came, day after day, and the grass grew fresh, and green, and sweet.

hillside, which was half of a great basin in the hills. Bel Bel and Mirri checked the foals at the edge of the tree line.

"Never run out into clear country without first taking a very good look," they warned.

The foals could see nothing except steep snowgrass and rocks dropping down, down beyond their sight, and away over opposite a rough, timbered hillside.

"That's where we will spend some of the summer," Bel Bel said. "It is too rough for the men and their cattle, but we get a good picking there."

Neither Thowra nor Storm knew what she meant.

"Down there," said Mirri, "is the Crackenback River. A nice, cool stream to drink at on hot days, and good sandy beaches, in places, for young ones to roll on."

They moved out on to the clear hillside, but never went far from the shelter of the trees. Thowra and Storm were too pleasantly tired to want to play and soon dropped to sleep in the sunshine. Bel Bel and Mirri grazed contentedly, a little distance off. All was quiet. There was the far-off sound of the river, running full and strong with water from the melted snows, and the sounds of kurrawongs, but otherwise a profound silence. Even the mares had grown sleepy, when all of a sudden there was a shrill whinny of fear from Thowra.

Bel Bel whipped round in time to see Thowra and Storm leaping up from their sleep, and there, grabbing at Thowra as he leapt, was a man. She neighed, calling her foal to come quickly, and started galloping towards them, ready to strike at the man. The foals, with long legs flailing, were racing towards her, wild with fear.

She heard Mirri scream with rage behind her. Then the man turned and ran into the trees.

The mares stopped in their headlong chase to snuff their trembling foals all over and make sure they were unhurt.

Bel Bel was all for chasing the man.

"He was no stockman, he had no whip," she said.

"No," answered Mirri, "but even a man alone, walking through the mountains, sometimes has a gun. No, we will thankfully take our foals and go." She turned to Storm. "See, my son, that was a man. Never go near Man, nor his huts, nor his yards where he fences in cattle and his own tame horse. Man will hurt you and capture you; put straps of leather rope upon your head, tie you up, fence you in, beat you if you bite or kick…" She was sweating with fear as she spoke, and the two foals' trembling increased.

"And you, Thowra," said Bel Bel. "I told you you would have to be as fleet as the wind. For your creamy coat and your silver mane and tail they will hunt you, so that they may ride astride your back over your own mountains. Beware of Man!"

Still sweating with fear, the two mares led their foals away, slipping like wraiths between the trees, trotting steeply down, trotting, trotting.

After quite a long way they were getting near the head of the stream. Here the mares went more slowly, stopping to sniff the air.

"It is from this hut he must have come, but he is not back yet," Bel Bel said.

"There may be others," Mirri's nostrils were quivering.

"I can smell no fresh smoke."

"But, still, let us drop much lower down and cross the stream there, rather than follow the track near the hut."

Bel Bel rubbed one ear on a foreleg.

"The foals are very tired," she said. "We had better spend the night near water. A drink for us will make more milk for them too."

They slept that evening well below the head of the Crackenback, with the singing stream beside them, but occasionally when the north wind blew, the two mares would wrinkle their nostrils and mutter between their teeth, "Smoke!" So when the moon rose, they nosed the foals up on their tired legs and started the long climb up Dead Horse Ridge.

Bel Bel whipped round in time to see Thowra and Storm leaping up from their sleep, and there, grabbing at Thowra as he leapt, was a man.

Once on top they could afford to rest again, but it took the poor foals hours to climb it, and when they found a soak of water to drink, just beyond the top, the mares let the little ones drop down on the soft ground and sleep undisturbed till daybreak.

From there on the travelling was easy, and Bel Bel and Mirri were not so anxious. They were a long way from the hut, and getting very close to the wild horses' winter and spring grazing grounds where, until the snows had all gone, they were never bothered by men.

It was evening when the four of them looked down into a narrow valley off the Cascades, and saw their own herd grazing. Just then the great golden chestnut stallion, leader of the herd, raised his head and saw them and let out a shrill trumpeting cry of greeting.

The two mares neighed in reply and started trotting down the long slope, followed by their nervous foals.

*It was evening when the four of them looked down into a
narrow valley off the Cascades, and saw their own herd grazing.*

WILD HORSES

Herds of wild horses roam free in many parts of the world – from mustangs on America's vast plains, to Asiatic wild horses on the central Asian steppes, to Brumbies in the Australian outback. Horses were first introduced to Australia in 1788. By 1860, many of these domesticated horses had escaped into the bush and become wild. There are probably as many as 600,000 wild Brumbies in Australia today.

Brumbies have highly developed survival instincts, including a strong fear of snakes.

Going for gold
After gold was discovered in southeast Australia in 1851, many horse breeders rushed into mining, leaving thousands of abandoned horses to join herds of wild Brumbies.

On the wild side
Food was scarce in the bush, and Brumbies became smaller than domestic horses. But they developed a survival instinct that enabled them to withstand their harsh environment.

Herd instinct
Like all wild horses, Brumbies live in herds. Each herd is led by a mature stallion, which protects its mares and foals from danger.

Hunted down
Stockmen (Australian cowboys) could not tame Brumbies, so tried to hunt them off their lands. By the 1960s the large numbers of Brumbies being killed caused concern worldwide. Today, strict laws limit Brumby hunting.

PEGASUS

by Roger Lancelyn Green

Pegasus was the winged horse of Prince Bellerophon. This is the story of how Bellerophon captured him in order to kill the Chimera, a monster with a lion's head, a goat's body and a dragon's tail.

After many, many days he [Bellerophon] came to the island where the wise man Polyidus lived, and begged him to tell him how the Chimera might be overcome.

"My son," said Polyidus solemnly, "there is no man walking on the ground who can come near to the Chimera and live, nor is there any four-footed creature on earth."

"Why then," exclaimed Bellerophon in dismay, "only the birds could come near it, and there is no bird strong enough for me to ride on."

"No bird," said Polyidus, "but there is the hippogryph – the flying horse – a great white steed with wings whose home is upon the magic mountain where the nine singing Fairies, called Muses, have their home. Only if you can catch and ride the hippogryph, whose name is Pegasus, can you overcome the Chimera. And even so, you must remember that no weapon can pierce him to the heart."

So Prince Bellerophon set sail for the land of Greece, and in time he came to the magic mountain, and found the singing Fairies seated round the moon-shaped spring of water which Pegasus had made with a stamp of his hoof.

They greeted Bellerophon kindly, but when he told them why he had come, they shook their heads and looked grave.

"Pegasus the flying horse does come to drink at this fountain," they said. "But no mortal can ride him, nor do we know of any magic to catch a hippogryph – the fleetest of creatures that tread the earth, and of any that fly through the air."

Bellerophon was in despair. But nevertheless he lay down that night beside the magic fountain, hiding among the grass and flowers as best he could, and determined to keep awake and try to catch Pegasus.

In spite of all his efforts, however, he fell suddenly into a deep sleep. And as he slept a vivid dream came to him. He dreamt that he woke, still lying beside the magic fountain, and saw a shining form standing above him – as of a great Queen who wore a shining shield on her arm and a golden helmet on her head. In her hand she carried a bridle made of gold, and this she held out to him, saying: "Do you sleep, you who may be King of Lycia one day? Rather awake, be ready, and take this which I bring you – the charm to tame your steed – on which no other mortal shall ever ride!"

Then Bellerophon woke [in real fact] and as he looked about him, he saw something glimmering in the grass beside his hand – the golden bridle which he had seen in his dream.

Scarcely had he taken it in his hands when he heard the swish of mighty wings, and the great white hippogryph came gliding down in the moonlight until he stood near him, neighing and arching his neck.

...a great Queen who wore a shining shield on her arm and a golden helmet on her head.

Then, folding his wings along his sides, he stepped forward and put down his nose into the silver waters of the fountain to drink.

Very cautiously Bellerophon crept forward on his hands and knees until he was right under the outstretched neck. Then suddenly he slipped the golden bit into the open mouth, and rising to his feet slid the bridle-straps over the snow-white ears and with a quick movement passed the golden chain under his neck and clipped it into place. Then, as Pegasus tossed his head in the air with a sudden snort, Bellerophon flung the reins back over his head and sprang onto his back.

In a moment they were off the ground and speeding away through the night, far over the dark mountains and the deep seas.

Prince Bellerophon shouted aloud with joy in that great, mad flight, and Pegasus his winged horse neighed and tossed his head.

In the dawning they landed upon another hill-top above an isthmus between two gulfs of the sea, and here Pegasus stamped with his hoof once more, and another fountain gushed out, at which both he and his rider drank.

Then Bellerophon slipped out the bit so that Pegasus could graze, and the great winged horse

Very cautiously Bellerophon crept forward on his hands and knees...

neighed in a friendly manner and rubbed his nose against his rider's shoulder.

Now that he had his steed, Prince Bellerophon set out in search of the fierce Chimera. At last he came upon her ravaging through the fruitful valleys, devouring the sheep and cattle, and destroying with her fiery breath all that stood in her way.

Flying high over it in the air, Bellerophon began shooting at the creature with sharp arrows. But although these wounded her, they did not seem able to do her any real harm, and merely made her far more furious and destructive.

Roaring loudly the Chimera bounded about, breathing great tongues of flame through her goat's

Now that he had his steed, Prince Bellerophon set out in search of the fierce Chimera. At last he came upon her.

mouth which stuck upon a long neck from the middle of her back. As he swooped down on Pegasus, Bellerophon felt the heat of that deadly breath, and an idea came to him.

Away he soared on Pegasus, and presently came flying back again with his long spear held firmly in both hands, and on the point of it a great lump of lead. Down over the Chimera he swooped on Pegasus, and as the terrible creature opened her goat-mouth to breathe out a great tongue of fire, Bellerophon dropped the lump of lead down her throat.

Then the Chimera roared and rolled and writhed on the ground, clawing at herself with her lion's talons and her dragon's claws. For the lump of lead melted in her burning throat, and the molten metal went trickling down into her entrails and her stomach, and searing its way through her until it reached her heart.

And then the Chimera rolled over for the last time, and lay still and dead.

*And then the Chimera rolled over for the last time,
and lay still and dead.*

HORSES IN ANCIENT GREECE

Horses not only played an important part in Greek mythology but were also central to life in ancient Greece. Pictures of horses and chariots on vases from 1550–1500 BC suggest a society in which the horse was crucial to battle, worship and sport. However, because of the unsuitable natural environment, the Greeks had to rely on horses from neighbouring areas to improve their native breeds.

Warfare
In early Greek warfare, horses were used to pull chariots to battle. Later, mounted troops crossed Greece's mountainous terrain.

The myth of Pegasus emphasises the close relationship between man and horse. Prince Bellerophon can only defeat the Chimera with the help of Pegasus.

Sports
Chariot racing was a national sport in ancient Greece. The first chariot races were for four-horse chariots, and were held at the Olympic Games in 680 BC.

Worship
Although the horse itself was not worshipped, its image was used to represent gods and goddesses who were worshipped. This statue of a horse head comes from a temple dedicated to the goddess Demeter, the goddess of women, marriage and agriculture. She was often represented by a black mare's head.

Breeding
The Pindos is directly descended from the old Thessalonian horse bred in ancient Greece. Noted by the Greek poet, Oppian (c.AD211), for its "beauty, courage and endurance", today the pony is used as a pack pony in the mountains, for light farm work and forestry.

A FOAL FOR CANDY

from the novel by Diana Pullein-Thompson

*Based on Diana Pullein-Thompson's real experience of
witnessing the birth of a foal, this is a moving account
of a foal's unexpected arrival into the world.*

I woke up. It was dark. A little rain spattered the window pane. My first thought was for Candy. I turned over and tried to be calm. "Briony checked her at midnight," I told myself. "But we should have brought her to the home field. The vet said…" The house was very quiet. The silence was beautiful in the soft summer night. The rain had stopped now and I could smell the lavender bush which grew at the bottom of my window. For the hundredth time I wished I had a dog lying at the end of my bed or in a basket nearby. I needed a being with whom I could discuss my fears. In this way I might have cleared my mind.

"Half an hour's delay can be as dangerous for a foaling mare as two hours for a cow."

Where had I read that? I turned over again and switched on the light, which immediately attracted a sand-coloured moth. I dragged my watch from under my pillow – ten past one. If she foaled disastrously tonight and died I should never forgive myself. It could be that some strange telepathy between Candy and myself had wakened me, a message moving like a spirit across the great darkness of the night. My imagination soared; fearful pictures ran before my mind like a horror film.

My mother once told me that it was the things you hadn't done which you regretted in later life. "Too late," she declared, were the saddest words in the English language. I got up, pulled jeans over my pyjamas, put on a sweater and crept downstairs. I picked up a heavy

My mother once told me that it was the things you hadn't done which you regretted in later life.

rubber-clad torch, pushed my bare feet into boots and slipped out into the cool darkness.

Walking down the lane, I was conscious of charcoal clouds moving across an immeasurable sky, and trees standing still like stones. The world was suddenly a stage waiting for lights, actors, and audience to bring it to life.

"Candy?"

"Are you all right?" I was astonished at my matter-of-fact tone of voice as I trapped Candy in my torch's beam and saw her flared nostrils, her wild eyes, and sweat-soaked neck. I held out my arms as though I could catch her in them like a frightened child, but she flung herself at my feet with a groan, her sides heaving, her stomach enormous, her hoofs churning the grass into mud as her panting turned into squeaks which seemed extraordinary coming from so large an animal. I had a picture in my mind from a veterinary book of how a foal should arrive; forelegs first with the head resting on them, and now, looking at Candy, I knew something was wrong. For in the torchlight I saw that one hoof was pushing in the wrong place, causing a red, ball-like bulge under her tail. My instinct was to stay and comfort and help her, but common sense bade me run. I vaulted the gate, pelted down the road, my heart thudding, and reached the house.

"Wake up everyone! Candy is foaling and everything's going wrong – everything." There was a trace of panic in my voice, because as usual I feared the worst. Briony keeps the vet's number on a card for emergencies, so I soon got through to the surgery, where a recording instructed me where to phone to reach the vet on duty. Next I had to look up a code, and by the time I had done that, David, my brother, and Briony were downstairs putting on shoes.

Sleepily, Thelma Wright, our nicest vet, said she would come at once. I grabbed a headcollar and tore back to the field with Briony following with sterilized string and scissors in case the navel cord needed tying and cutting.

Candy was lying on the ground with her teeth bared.

"She could die," I said dramatically.

"Calm down!" cried my sister. "You won't make a vet if you overreact. David, please will you run back and bring a bucket of warm water with antiseptic and the Vaseline if you can find it?"

Then our parents arrived.

"She looks in a bad way," Mother said.

"She could die," I repeated. "Foaling mares die more easily than calving cows. I've read it up."

"We're more likely to lose the foal than the mare," my sister told me. "I wish David would hurry."

"And Thelma Wright. What on earth is Thelma Wright doing?" I asked, kneeling down by Candy's head.

"Better fetch Fred," Dad suggested, as those terrible squeaks of pain started again. "He said he worked on a Canadian stud farm."

"She's pushing for all she's worth, but the foal's stuck. There's no time to waste and he's the only person nearby who might know what to do," Mother agreed.

"But he hates us," I cried seeing again those angry, glittering eyes at the door of the tack room, the gun glinting under his arm. "He thinks I'm a nosey parker."

"Oh, forget that! Don't hang around or you'll have a dead foal on your hands," Dad said. "Even I can see that, and the mare's in pain."

"Fred may hate you, but he loves animals, there's no doubt about that," Mother added.

"Go on, Lynne," urged Briony.

"No, I'm staying with Candy. I'm scared of Fred. Please go, Briony. Please be quick. I'm sure the foal needs turning round or something."

Briony ran. Candy scrambled to her feet, circled twice and collapsed on the ground again.

"Labour pains. You've got to expect labour pains," Mother said.

David came back across the field with a bucket and a hurricane lamp.

"One hoof must be in the wrong place. They should come out side by side," I explained. "Whoa, Candy! Gently, Candy! Help is coming."

Then David came back across the field with a bucket and a hurricane lamp. "We need more light on the scene. How is she?"

"Terrible. Do you think I could turn the hoof around?"

"No, you could do more damage. Better wait for Briony," Dad said.

"But Briony doesn't know everything," I insisted. "It's all happening too high up."

"She knows more than you," Mother said. "She's older."

"Lynne, you're overdramatizing again," David muttered gently.

"I don't know," Mother said. "She does look rather miserable and we're standing round like a load of half wits. If policemen can deliver babies, why can't we deliver the foal?"

"Give me the bucket, please," I cried.

I plunged my hands into the water, put Vaseline on my arms and tried what I had seen a vet do on television, but I couldn't get a hand inside.

"She does look rather miserable and we're standing round like a load of half wits."

Then Briony came back. "Fred's getting dressed. What are you doing, Lynne? Move over, let me have a go."

She took off her coat, rolled up her sleeves, applied Vaseline and soap, and disinfected her hands, but she was no more successful than I had been. "I can't. There seems no room. She closes up on me," she complained.

"Come on now, make way. Where's the soap? We'll soon put things right." Fred had arrived. He flung his coat down. "Hoof pushing against rectum. Could be serious. Must hurry," he added. "I've turned plenty of foals round in my time. You don't need no vet. Whoa, little lady! Steady there!"

He brought out his hands and washed them in the water. "She'll be all right now. I've straightened the hoof. It's beside its mate now. The birth will be normal."

"Why couldn't I do it?" Briony asked.

"You have to time it right, push in a hand between the heaves. I've turned sheep and cattle too. It's easy once you know," Fred beamed.

"Here comes the vet," shouted David. "I'll open the gate."

"Late as usual," growled Fred.

"That's not fair," Mother said.

"I went to your house. You should have told me where the mare was," Thelma Wright complained.

"My fault. I'm terribly sorry," I said, chastened.

"Then I saw the lights. I really only lost five minutes."

Now the vet's car lamps lit up the whole scene. Candy looked around, her cheeks pinched with pain, her nostrils still flared, milk running from her teats.

"Hoof pushing against rectum. I brought it down. Look, foal's coming now," Fred said, as Thelma Wright sprang from her car.

She took one hoof and Fred the other and, pulling gently, they brought out the foal, long, wet, and dark as the night.

"It's a fine one," Fred said.

After Thelma Wright had injected mare and foal with an antibiotic and anti-tetanus serum, she left to see a sick cow and we stood in an admiring circle to watch Candy, who prodded her foal with a hoof.

"Don't, you'll hurt him," I objected.

"That's normal, that is. Wants to see what he's made of," Fred told us. "Go on, old lady, get the little devil moving." The next moment Candy was guiding the foal in a circle with her knees.

"He's got to stand before he can suck. Well, I'm going back to my warm bed." Fred turned away.

We looked at each other, searching for words. It's hard to express gratitude to someone for whom you feel no affection.

"We're enormously grateful. You saved the foal," Briony began rather formally. "The vet might have been too late. We can't thank you enough."

"It's not the first and I dare say it won't be the last. You've got a nice colt there, well bred I would say."

"Well, good night," said Mother. "We're all grateful to you. I'm off to bed as well."

"Me too," Dad said. "What a night!"

The adults walked away, apart from Briony, whom we never think of as grown up, but merely as one of us with just a bit more authority.

But our troubles weren't over.

"We've got to get him sucking. The first milk's very important," Briony said. "See if you can guide his mouth to the udder, Lynne."

David held the hurricane lamp so that a shaft of light fell between Candy's hind legs, but when I got the foal's mouth in the right place, he only fumbled clumsily, too weak to draw the milk and too stupid to bend his head in the right direction.

"It's because he's had a difficult birth," my sister announced at last. "Who in this village has a baby's bottle?"

"Mirabelle's parents' housekeeper has a baby boy," David replied promptly. "I've seen the girl stuff a bottle in the child's mouth when he keeps crying. I'll go and wake Mirabelle if you like."

"It's half past two – an awful time to drag someone out of bed, but we can't leave this little guy without milk," Briony said. "He'll get weaker and weaker if he doesn't take the milk soon. There's not a lot of time. David, do you think…"

"Yes, all right. I'll go, of course, but I just hope I don't wake up Mirabelle's parents."

"We'll leave you in charge, Lynne. Here's the torch. We'll take the lamp."

The faint squelch of their feet on the grass died away. The charcoal clouds moved silently across the ink-black sky. Candy lay there, looking like a pale Chinese porcelain horse, with her foal folded up at her side. I wanted to sit down then to share their peacefulness.

Soon David, Mirabelle and Briony came striding back across the field.

"You've got a nice colt there, well bred I would say."

"All sterilized and clean!" Briony waved a baby's plastic bottle. "Up you get, Candy! Come on!" She pushed the cream body with her foot.

"Oh, what a pity to move them when they look so comfortable," cried Mirabelle. "Why don't you leave them? What a dear little foal! I'm so glad you woke me."

"He must suck or his insides won't function properly," Briony said sternly. Then she started to milk the mare.

After much persuasion, the foal took two pulls from the bottle and then gave up. "Not enough," my sister said. "We must persevere."

So we went on trying until a skein of pale grey unwove its thin strands across the sky, spreading soft light across the darkness.

"He's not going to suck – any fool can see that," David said flatly.

"Well, now it's light I shall ring the vet again. There's no other way," Briony said.

Half an hour later, Thelma Wright fed the foal by tube. I poured Candy's milk from a plastic jug down a funnel attached to the tube, which had been inserted though the foal's left nostril and ran right down into his stomach.

"There, now. He'll be all right," Thelma Wright said when the jug was empty.

And within minutes, the foal was up and walking on his long, wobbly legs. Soon afterwards the vet removed the tube and the long night was over.

*...Thelma Wright fed the foal by tube. I poured Candy's milk
from a plastic jug down a funnel attached to the tube,
which had been inserted though the foal's left nostril...*

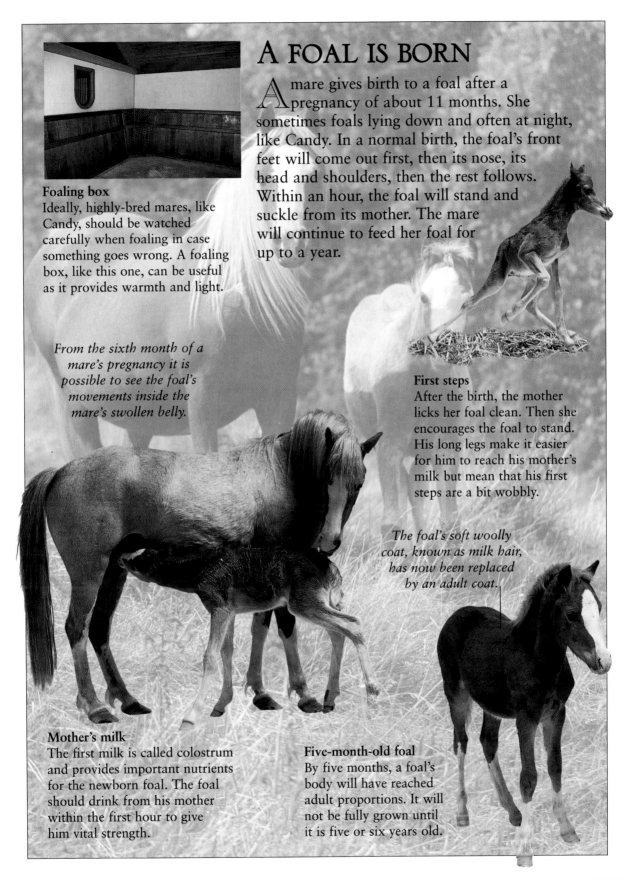

A FOAL IS BORN

A mare gives birth to a foal after a pregnancy of about 11 months. She sometimes foals lying down and often at night, like Candy. In a normal birth, the foal's front feet will come out first, then its nose, its head and shoulders, then the rest follows. Within an hour, the foal will stand and suckle from its mother. The mare will continue to feed her foal for up to a year.

Foaling box
Ideally, highly-bred mares, like Candy, should be watched carefully when foaling in case something goes wrong. A foaling box, like this one, can be useful as it provides warmth and light.

From the sixth month of a mare's pregnancy it is possible to see the foal's movements inside the mare's swollen belly.

First steps
After the birth, the mother licks her foal clean. Then she encourages the foal to stand. His long legs make it easier for him to reach his mother's milk but mean that his first steps are a bit wobbly.

The foal's soft woolly coat, known as milk hair, has now been replaced by an adult coat.

Mother's milk
The first milk is called colostrum and provides important nutrients for the newborn foal. The foal should drink from his mother within the first hour to give him vital strength.

Five-month-old foal
By five months, a foal's body will have reached adult proportions. It will not be fully grown until it is five or six years old.

MY BREAKING IN

from *Black Beauty* by Anna Sewell

Published in 1877, Black Beauty *was the first ever story to be written from a horse's point of view. Never before had readers been able to understand what it must be like to be so dependent on human beings, whether cruel or kind. In this extract, Black Beauty's owner decides it's time his four-year-old started to learn about the realities of life...*

I was now beginning to grow handsome; my coat had grown fine and soft, and was bright black. I had one white foot, and a pretty white star on my forehead. I was thought very handsome; my master would not sell me till I was four years old; he said lads ought not to work like men, and colts ought not to work like horses till they were grown up.

When I was four years old, Squire Gordon came to look at me. He examined my eyes, my mouth, and my legs; and then I had to walk and trot and gallop before him; he seemed to like me, and said, "When he has been well broken in, he will do very well." My master said he would break me in himself, as he should not like me to be frightened or hurt, and he lost no time about it, the next day he began.

My master said he would break me in himself... and he lost no time about it, the next day he began.

Every one may not know what breaking in is, therefore I will describe it. It means to teach a horse to wear a saddle and bridle and carry on his back a man, woman, or child; to go just the way they wish, and to go quietly. Besides this, he has to learn to wear a collar, a crupper, and a breeching, and to stand still whilst they are put on; then to have a cart or a chaise fixed behind him, so that he cannot walk or trot without dragging it after him: and he must go fast or slow, just as his driver wishes. He must never start at what he sees, nor speak to other horses, nor bite, nor kick, nor have any will of his own; but always do his master's will, even though he may be very tired or hungry; but the worst of all is, when his harness is once on, he may neither jump for joy nor lie down for weariness. So you see this breaking in is a great thing.

I had of course long been used to a halter and a headstall, and to be led about in the field and lanes quietly, but now I was to have a bit and a bridle; my master gave me some oats as usual, and after a good deal of coaxing, he got the bit into my mouth, and the bridle fixed, but it was a nasty thing! Those who have never had a bit in their mouths cannot think how bad it feels; a great piece of cold, hard steel as thick as a man's finger to be pushed into one's mouth, between one's teeth and over one's tongue, with the ends coming out at the corner of your mouth and held fast there by straps over your head, under your throat, round your nose, and under your chin; so that no way in the world can you get rid of the nasty hard thing; it is very bad! Yes, very bad! At least I thought so; but I knew my mother always wore one when she went out, and all horses did when they were grown up; and so, what with the nice oats, and what with my master's pats, kind words, and gentle ways, I got to wear my bit and bridle.

Next came the saddle, but that was not half so bad; my master put it on my back very gently, whilst old Daniel held my head; he then made the girths fast under my body, patting and talking to me all the time; then I had a few oats, then a little leading about, and this he did every day till I began to look for the oats and saddle. At length, one morning my master got on my back and rode me round the meadow on the soft grass.

It certainly did feel queer; but I must say I felt rather proud to carry my master, and as he continued to ride me a little every day, I soon became accustomed to it.

The next unpleasant business was putting on the iron shoes; that too was very hard at first. My master went with me to the smith's forge, to see that I was not hurt or got any fright. The blacksmith took my feet in his hand one after the other, and cut away some of the hoof. It did not pain me, so I stood still on three legs till he had done them all. Then he took a piece of iron the shape of my foot, and clapped it on, and drove some nails through the shoe quite into my hoof, so that the shoe was firmly on. My feet felt very stiff and heavy, but in time I got used to it.

And now having got so far, my master went on to break me to harness; there were more new things to wear. First, a stiff heavy collar just on my neck, and a bridle with great side-pieces against my eyes called blinkers and blinkers indeed they were, for I could not see on either side, but only straight in front of me; next there was a small saddle with a nasty stiff strap that went right under my tail; that was the crupper. I hated the crupper – to have my long tail doubled up and poked through that strap was almost as bad as the bit. I never felt more like kicking, but of course I could not kick such a good master, and so in time I got used to everything, and could do my work as well as my mother.

I must not forget to mention one part of my training, which I have always considered a very great advantage. My master sent me for a fortnight to a neighbouring farmer's, who had a meadow which was skirted on one side by a railway. There were some sheep and cows, and I was turned in amongst them.

I shall never forget the first train that ran by. I was feeding quietly

The next unpleasant business was putting on the iron shoes...

near the pales which separated the meadow from the railway, when
I heard a strange sound at a distance, and before I knew whence it came
– with a rush and a clatter, and a puffing out of smoke – a long black
train of something flew by, and was gone almost before I could draw my
breath. I turned, and galloped to the further side of the meadow

*…a long black train
of something flew by,
and was gone almost
before I could draw
my breath. I turned,
and galloped…*

as fast as I could go, and there I stood snorting with astonishment and fear. In the course of the day many other trains went by, some more slowly; these drew up at the station close by, and sometimes made an awful shriek and groan before they stopped. I thought it very dreadful, but the cows went on eating very quietly, and hardly raised their heads as the black frightful thing came puffing and grinding past.

For the first few days I could not feed in peace; but as I found that this terrible creature never came into the field, or did me any harm, I began to disregard it, and very soon I cared as little about the passing of a train as the cows and sheep did.

Since then I have seen many horses much alarmed and restive at the sight or sound of a steam engine; but thanks to my good master's care, I am as fearless at railway stations as in my own stable.

Now if anyone wants to break in a young horse well, that's the way.

Besides this, he has to have a cart or a chaise fixed behind him,
so that he cannot walk or trot without dragging it after him.

BREAKING IN

The term "breaking in" is a negative way of describing the taming of a horse as it suggests the horse's spirit must be broken. When Anna Sewell wrote *Black Beauty*, many cruel methods were used to break the animal's wild spirit. Today, people believe that the most effective way to tame a horse is with patience and understanding. The process is now called "making" a horse.

Saddle
The kindest way to get a horse used to the feel of a saddle is to place it on his back without a rider at first.

Harness
In Victorian times, working horses like Black Beauty, had to learn to wear a harness instead of a saddle, to pull carts or carriages.

Bridle
A steel bit and bridle are used to give the rider more control of the horse. Black Beauty finds the bit uncomfortable at first.

Wearing shoes
Fitting a horse with metal shoes is done by a blacksmith. The shoes prevent a horse's hooves from being damaged on hard roads.

Horse shoe and nails

A headcollar is used to make handling a horse easier.

The gentle touch
A horse that is treated with gentleness and kindness will always respond better to its rider.

ALICE AND THE WHITE KNIGHT

From *Alice Through the Looking Glass* by Lewis Carroll

During her adventures beyond the large mirror in her drawing-room, Alice encounters the bumbling White Knight, who promises to escort her through a wood. Alice soon notices that there is something rather odd about him – he seems quite unable to stay on his horse!

Alice walked on in silence, every now and then stopping to help the poor Knight, who certainly was not a good rider. Whenever the horse stopped (which it did very often), he fell off in front; and whenever it went on again (which it generally did rather suddenly), he fell off behind. Otherwise he kept on pretty well, except that he had a habit of now and then falling off sideways; and, as he generally did this on the side on which Alice was walking, she soon found that it was the best plan not to walk quite so close to the horse.

"I'm afraid you've not had much practice in riding," she ventured to say, as she was helping him up from his fifth tumble.

The Knight looked very much surprised, and a little offended at the remark. "What makes you say that?" he asked, as he scrambled back into the saddle, keeping hold of Alice's hair with one hand, to save himself from falling over on the other side.

"Because people don't fall off so often, when they've had practice."

"I've had plenty of practice," the Knight said very gravely, "plenty of practice!"

Alice could think of nothing better to say than "Indeed?" but she said it as heartily as she could. They went on a little way in silence after this, the Knight with his eyes shut, muttering to himself, and Alice watching anxiously for the next tumble.

"The great art of riding," the Knight suddenly began in a loud voice, waving his right arm as he spoke, "is to keep . . ." Here the sentence ended as suddenly as it had begun, as the Knight fell heavily on the top of his head exactly in the path where Alice was walking. She was quite frightened this time, and said in an anxious tone, as she picked him up, "I hope no bones are broken?"

"None to speak of," the Knight said, as if he didn't mind breaking two or three of them. "The great art of riding, as I was saying is – to keep your balance properly. Like this, you know . . ."

He let go the bridle, and stretched out both his arms to show Alice what he meant, and this time he fell flat on his back, right under the horse's feet.

"The great art of riding, as I was saying
is – to keep your balance properly."

*"Plenty of practice!"
he went on
repeating.*

"Plenty of practice!" he went on repeating, all the time that Alice was getting him on his feet again. "Plenty of practice!"

"It's too ridiculous!" cried Alice, losing all her patience this time. "You ought to have a wooden horse on wheels, that you ought!"

"Does that kind go smoothly?" the Knight asked in a tone of great interest, clasping his arms round the horse's neck as he spoke, just in time to save himself from tumbling off again.

"Much more smoothly than a live horse," Alice said, with a little scream of laughter, in spite of all she could do to prevent it.

"I'll get one," the Knight said thoughtfully to himself. "One or two – several."

*"You ought to have a
wooden horse on wheels,
that you ought!"*

BASIC RIDING TECHNIQUE

Despite his inability to stay "on board", the White Knight is quite right about the essential art of riding: keeping your balance. When you learn to ride, your first lesson will probably concentrate purely on your "seat" – the way you sit in your saddle. It's not as easy as it looks, but there are many exercises that you can do to give you confidence in the saddle, and help you keep your balance.

Sitting in the saddle
The correct position for a well-balanced seat is to sit deep in the saddle, back straight, head up, thighs and knees pressed down.

Round the world
This is a very good exercise for learning how to keep your balance in the saddle. First, holding on to the saddle, swing your right leg over the front of the saddle, so you face sideways. Next, move your left leg over the back of the saddle so you face the pony's tail. Carry on until you face forwards again.

Leaning back
Keeping your feet in the stirrups, but letting go of the reins, slowly lean back until you are lying on the pony's back. Then sit up again.

Swinging arms
With your feet in the stirrups, lift up your arms to shoulder level. Then turn your body from the waist to one side, then the other.

Toe touching
In this exercise you lean down to touch your left foot with your right hand and then your right foot with your left hand.

THE CHAMPIONS

by Monica Edwards

Nowadays draught horses are sadly becoming a rarer and rarer sight. In this story, Tess and John try to raise enough money to save two prize-winning Shire horses, Flower and Captain, from the slaughter-house.

John Thatcher and his sister Tess were running down the track to Manor Farm. It was not to see the farmer, who wasn't the sort of man anybody would see on purpose, or to see his wife, who was chronically sad. They were looking for Walter Pooley, the horseman.

"If only it hadn't been for school," John was saying as they ran, "we could have watched the ploughing match ourselves. I wonder why they always hold it in term time?"

"I'll bet Walter won his class, anyway," Tess said, "and the championship, too. He nearly always has, as well as dozens in other places."

"But it gets more difficult every year, with all the modern hydraulic-lift tractors. Walter's almost the only horse team left."

They climbed the gate into the farmyard and crossed a stretch of concrete to the stable. It was quite clearly a stable, because of the halter thrown over the open half-door, and the sounds and smells of horses coming out of it. The powerful brown hind view of one of its inhabitants filled the doorway like a picture in a frame.

"Oh, hullo, young uns," said Walter Pooley. He had one hand, with a curry comb in it, resting on a grey horse's rump, and the other was grooming its flank in long, strong strokes that sent fine dust floating in a shaft of low sunlight.

*The powerful black hind view of one of its inhabitants
filled the doorway like a picture in a frame.*

"Hullo, Walter!" Tess and John glanced round at once to look at the shining bridles where they hung on pegs along the wall. On one of them a crisp, red rosette was tied, but, far more important than this, there was a new card at the end of the row of prize-cards that were tacked underneath the bridles, and it said on it, "Champion; Finkley and District Ploughing Match".

"Walter! You've won it again!"

"That's right, Flower and Captain's won it again. Dah! Those

"Those stinking tractors haven't got nothing on a real pair of horses," said Walter proudly.

stinking tractors haven't got nothing on a real pair of horses," said Walter proudly, but there was a kind of sadness in the pride in his voice. John supposed it was sadness for the passing of the heyday of great horses, and said, "Well anyway, there'll always be a rear horse-team while you and Flower and Captain are around," to cheer him up.

"Ah," said Walter non-committally, and then, "This one made the 99th prize and the eleventh championship, all with Flower and Captain. Pity it's the last match this year, ain't it, Flower, old girl? I'd like to've made the century; and even better, the dozen."

"You'll easily do it next year," Tess said. "May I give them a sugar-lump each, for winning? And one for Prince, to make it fair."

"Carry on," said Walter, moving over with his brushes and curry comb to Captain, who was a perfect match for Flower except that his dappling was a little darker, and his build a little heavier. "But as to next year who's to know where me and the horses'll be? Manor Farm's been sold, just like that, over all our heads and no warning."

"Walter – no!" Tess and John stared at him.

"I seen the new man down here two or three times, never dreaming what he were here for. But the boss, he tells me they clinched the deal this morning, while I were ploughing."

"But can't you stay on with the new man – you and the horses?" John asked. "I should think he'd be glad to have a champion ploughman and a team like this."

"That's just where you're mistaken, son." Walter was brushing out Captain's silver main, still crinkly from the morning's festive plaits. "The new gent's mechanical. He don't hold with horses and that – like most of 'em today."

"Perhaps whoever buys the horses will take you on with them," John suggested. "They aren't likely to have a better ploughman."

Walter looked up at them starkly, over Captain's broad back. "No one buys horses much these days, least of all old horses. Prince, there, he'll likely go to some smallholder chap – he's young and useful. But Flower and Captain, they're rising 15 now, and they never worked for nobody but me. They wouldn't go kindly for a new horseman now, at their time of life."

Tess wiped her sugar-slobbery palm on a handful of straw. "But surely someone will pay something for Flower and Captain? Someone who sees what fine, beautiful horses they are, and who would be proud to have champions like them."

"Ah. Someone'll pay, you bet. And that'll be the slaughter merchants. Fine, big horses is what they like above anything."

John and Tess simply didn't believe what Walter said. They supposed he was exaggerating out of bitterness for what was going to happen. But Walter shook his head sadly. He brought his large hand down with a tender slap on Captain's rump and said: "We got about one month, me and the horses. Me to find another job – who wants a horseman, nowadays? – and the horses... well... Anyway," he added firmly, "they've had a good life. A good, long, useful life, and all the while they carried flying colours."

"Couldn't Flower and Captain retire? They jolly well deserve it, if any horses ever did."

"But it mustn't happen!" Tess said. "We'll have to do something – I don't know what, but there must be something. If they're too old and weak for anybody but you, Walter, what about the Homes of Rest for Horses? Couldn't Flower and Captain retire? They jolly well deserve it, if any horses ever did."

Walter nodded solemnly. "I daresay. I thought about that myself, but I reckon you got to pay to put horses in retirement. And another thing, even supposing some Home did offer to take 'em can you see the guv'nor letting 'em go, and not getting a penny back, when those slaughter gents'll put up around 40 or 50 quid apiece?"

"We got about one month, me and the horses. Me to find another job – who wants a horseman, nowadays?"

The slant of sunlight had gone from the stable window and soon it would be dusk. John and Tess patted the horses and picked up their satchels. "Cheer up Walter! Something will happen, I'm sure it will. We'll let you know the moment we've thought of anything."

But they couldn't do that, because when they thought of it they were on the bus on the way to school, the next morning. "What we've go to do," John said, "is collect money for buying the horses and paying for their retirement."

"But how much? And who from?"

"We'll find out how much. I'll write to one of the Homes. Then we'll have to try everyone we know, and start a proper Save the Horses Fund."

For the next few days they had no time at all for visiting the farm, except for one brief dash in and out to tell Walter the wonderful news that the Horses' Home had written to say that they would accept Flower and Captain for nothing at all, if necessary.

"Oh dear, it simply must be, now we've said so," Tess anxiously.

But by the end of the first week the Fund stood at only £15 2s. John and Tess went up to the farm on the Saturday morning to tell Walter that they were still pushing on.

"We must reach £80 somehow, and we're going to, however unlikely it looks now." Walter looked at them gravely over Captain's steaming back. The horses had just come in from the fields and were being unharnessed for the dinner hour.

"Look, young uns," he said gently, "you better forget that Fund, see. You can't make it now. The guv'nor, he fixed up with the slaughter men. £45 for Captain here, and £40 for Flower. Saturday noon."

"Oh Walter! But that's only in a week." Walter nodded, saying nothing. But after a minute he said suddenly and fiercely; "I won't let 'em have my horses, though. My horses go through their murder-sheds?" He looked at the three of them, the brown and the greys, lovingly. "That Prince, he's all right! Going to the brewery. But my greys…"

Then suddenly, during breakfast on Tuesday morning, the children's mother said, "You could try writing to the paper perhaps."

"What are you going to do, Walter?" Tess looked at him half hopefully, half apprehensively.

"I got me own gun," said Walter, with a strange kind of dignity. "I won't let 'em suffer. Sooner put 'em down myself merciful, I would, than let those pirates get a hand on them. And they can do what they like to me, afterwards. My horses've served me all their lives, and now I stand to serve them."

John and Tess were very shaken. Their chances of raising enough money to outbid the slaughterers before the following

Saturday were so small as to be almost hopeless.

"There must be a way," said John, "if only we can think of it."

But no one they knew seemed to be any better than they were at thinking of it. And the next two days at bob-a-jobbing only added a further £3 10s to the Fund, though everyone at both John's and Tess's schools had done their best.

Then suddenly, during breakfast on Tuesday morning, the children's mother said, "You could try writing to the paper perhaps."

"The paper? Gosh, yes, I suppose we could!" John said. "But do you think they'd put it in? Or that many people would help us if they did? I mean, Walter and the horses would be strangers to them."

But when they met in the bus, coming home again that evening, John said to Tess: "I wrote that letter to the paper. If they put it in, and anyone answers, we'll get the letters on Saturday morning."

"But Saturday morning is..." Tess began uncertainly. Then, "John! Listen! We must go to the farm at once and tell Walter to wait until after the post before – before..." her voice failed.

"At least an hour after the post, to give us time to get to the farm," John said. "But of course, the paper might not print my letter."

The paper did print it. John and Tess could hardly concentrate at all on Friday's lessons, because of wondering whether enough people could possibly, at that moment, be writing out enough cheques and postal orders to save the horses.

On Saturday morning the postman came up the path as usual and pushed two letters through the letter-box. They were both ordinary business circulars. John and Tess simply couldn't look at each other. Finishing breakfast was quite out of the question. Neither of them had felt so awful in all their lives. The morning began its heavy-footed, slow progress, until it was nearly three-quarters of an hour after the postman's visit. Tess wouldn't look at the clock, but John was looking at it all the time. Tess just stared hopelessly out of the window. And that was why she saw the red van first. It pulled up outside their gate, behind the hedge, and she could see a postman's cap bobbing along towards the

"A whole sack! Look, Tess. A sackful of letters, just for us!"

doors at the back of the van.

"John – it's a post office van!" she hardly dared hope. But John, dashing across to the window, felt that he had known all along that help must be coming – if only it came in time.

"A whole sack! Look, Tess. A sackful of letters, just for us!" They tore through the room and down the hall and opened the door.

"Too many for the postman's bicycle," grinned the man with the sack. "What've you started, then? A mail order business."

It was fifty minutes from the time of the first postman's visit. John's usually slow brain jumped to the only answer. "I say, sir! Could you possibly take the sack, and us with it to Manor Farm? Now, sir? You see, it's a matter of life and death."

"We can explain everything on the way," pleaded Tess.

The driver looked at them. "Right. Hop in," he said. "It's against regulations, but with life and death you've got to make allowances, eh?"

In less than two minutes John had him breaking further regulations, because he had never driven that van so fast before, in all his 12 years at the post office, and even up the bumpy track to Manor Farm they hardly slowed down. In the farmyard they threw themselves out as the van came to a stop and raced across the concrete to the stable.

"Walter!"

He was tying a white cloth around Flower's eyes.

"Walter! We've got a whole sackful of letters here, and probably every one with money in it. They came late, because there were so many. We brought them as quickly as we could."

Walter turned towards them with a slow, incredulous look; and then he slipped the bandage down from Flower's eyes. "A sackful, you said, eh?"

"We've got to count up and see how much there is, Walter. We'll need you to help."

It took them more than an hour and a half to make even a hurried, rough calculation. Every letter had to be opened, and the sum inside noted for sending letters of thanks. Then all had to be quickly added up: and the time was ticking towards noon in a way that made Tess's heart jump. The total was £94 7s. And the time was 11.45.

In the farmyard they threw themselves out as the van came to a stop and raced across the concrete to the stable.

"God bless us all, let's take it to the guv'nor quick!" said Walter.

"It's enough for buying the horses and paying their fare," said John, as they hurried to the farmhouse, "and with our own Fund added we'll be able to send quite a lot to the Horses Home, too, towards their keep."

And that, exciting though it was, was not quite the end; because one day in the next autumn, when Walter was visiting his horses, the manager of the Horses' Home said to him: "I suppose you know that the County Ploughing Match is being held in this village? Why not come over and enter Flower and Captain, just once more?"

And Walter did just that.

Tess and John still have the letter he wrote to them afterwards, which says: "I only wish you could have been there and seen my horses get their dozen and century! I reckon you'd have been as proud as I was, since, we'd never have done it, but for you."

"I only wish you could have been there and seen my horses get their dozen and century! I reckon you'd have been as proud as I was, since, we'd never have done it, but for you."

DRAUGHT HORSES

Flower and Captain are among the last in a great tradition of heavy working horses. Until the invention of the steam engine in the 1800s, the horse was the chief means of transport, and thus work on the farm. Today, tractors have taken the place of horses, though teams can still be seen at country shows.

City life
For most of the 19th century, public transport in the cities was provided by horse-drawn omnibuses. The work was so hard that a horse's working life was only four years.

Ploughing the fields
Before the invention of the tractor, farming depended on horses for ploughing the fields, and pulling hay carts and wagons. Most farm machinery could be pulled by a team of two horses, like Flower and Captain. But in the US, huge combine harvesters were pulled by teams of 40 horses.

Some breweries still use horse-drawn carts today.

For showing, the mane is plaited and decorated with ribbons to show the strong neck.

In industry
Draught horses were used in all forms of industry. They moved heavy machines, pulled coal wagons, even pulled the early trains.

Showing off
Although heavy horse breeds no longer play a significant role in farming, their strength and dignity still grace many shows.

The long hair around the feet is called feather.

POST TIME

from *The Black Stallion and the Girl* by Walter Farley

*Few writers have managed to convey the breathless thrills of horse-racing
more vividly than Walter Farley. In this extract from his* Black Stallion
*series of novels, the Black, with Alec on board, is attempting to
win the $50,000 Roseben handicap. It's a close-run thing…*

At Aqueduct, the following Saturday, the Black was saddled for
the feature race on the afternoon programme. Stripped of all
useless fat and flesh, he was in his finest shape.

He seemed to know he had never looked so handsome, for he feigned
impatience and rebellion against Alec, who stood at his head. The Black
pawed the ground and half-reared; his mane, so carefully brushed and
combed only moments before, fell tousled about his head and neck. The
pure curve of his high, crested neck arched majestically and his great eyes
flashed fire as he surveyed the other horses in the saddling paddock.

"Hold him still, won't you?" Henry Dailey said, tightening the girth
strap; his voice was gruff, as if speaking to an employee instead of to
Alec. Henry's forehead was so deeply wrinkled that his eyebrows were
separated from his grey hair only by a thin line of skin.

When the old man had the girth as he wanted it, he straightened and
placed a hand on the lead pad beneath the saddle.

"No horse should carry so much weight, but we'll show 'em. We're
dodging nobody."

Alec said not a word, knowing nothing was expected of him. Henry
was talking for his own benefit. The heavy weights that track
handicappers were assigning to the Black in every race he entered must
eventually set a turf record. They created a lot of tension before a race

*When the old man had the girth as he wanted it, he straightened
and placed a hand on the lead pad beneath the saddle.*

so Alec understood and tolerated his old friend's gruffness.

The weights were assigned in order to give every horse in a race a chance at first money. The impost each horse carried on his back was made by taking into consideration his race record, his workouts and his physical condition. Lead weights inserted in a pad beneath the saddle were added, when necessary, to the weight of the rider in order to meet the track handicapper's assigned impost. Champions carried the highest weights of all, and the Black was consistently carrying more weight than any other horse in racing.

Henry stepped back, a stocky man with a barrel-shaped chest. His eyes, like his mouth, were narrow slits in a round-cheeked face. His nose was his only prominent feature, being hooked, almost like the beak of a bird of prey. He examined the stallions's hocks and forelegs, the solidity of his flanks and chest, looking for any sign of soreness or weakness.

The paddock judge called, "Riders, mount your horses, please!"

Alec was boosted into the saddle and, picking up the reins, he spoke quietly to the Black. Once Alec was up, the stallion usually settled down, his nervousness being quickly replaced by an eagerness to get on with the business of racing. The Black didn't like to wait.

"Any instructions?" Alec asked Henry. The trainer had mounted Napoleon, their stable pony, and was accompanying them to the post.

The red-coated bugler stood in the middle of the track.

Henry shook his head. "Just ride your race," he said, grabbing the Black's bridle. "There's nothing I can tell you that you don't already know." He moved Napoleon's hindquarters between the Black and a horse following too closely behind.

The red-coated bugler, wearing shiny black boots and a black hunting cap, stood in the middle of the track, a long coach horn pressed to his lips. Henry shivered with anticipation at the sound of the call to the post. He had lost count of how many years ago it was that he had heard it for the first time. He was as old and grey and sway-backed as the gelding he rode, and just as fat. But each of them still had a job to do.

The great stands were packed and overflowing. Everybody was tense. Everybody was waiting. There were nine horses in the post parade for the Roseben Handicap, a distance of seven furlongs (seven-eighths of a mile), for a purse of $50,000. But the crowd saw only one entry, the Black.

Everybody knew the champion would not be found wanting in speed, but there was always racing luck to consider... plus the heavy impost of 138 pounds on his back against light-weighted horses, some carrying only 103 pounds. Besides, it was a short race for the Black. He might have trouble catching the others before the finish if his rider made a single mistake. There would be bumping and swerving in so large a field. So this might be a day to remember, the day the greatest handicap runner of all time was beaten, and they would have been there to see it!

Alec wrapped the reins about his hands. At the starting gate Henry left him. Between the Black's ears Alec could see the sun dropping behind the New York City skyscrapers to the west. He glanced at the other horses and had no fear of them. It was only their riders who could beat him. They were among the best in the business and capable of taking quick advantage of any mistake he might make, even helping him to make a big one that would cost the Black a victory.

They were on either side of him, milling behind the gate, awaiting assistant starters to lead their mounts into the padded, narrow stalls.

He glanced at the other horses and had no fear of them. It was only their riders who could beat him.

Each rode slowly, whip in hand and ready. Their faces disclosed no emotion. They all might have been carved of wood or cut from toughest leather. Their bodies were hard and fit beneath glossy silks; lips were thin and tightly clasped, looking cruel, as did their narrowed eyes.

"Get down to business," Alec cautioned himself. A moment later he rode the Black into the Number 1 stall. The other riders followed him into the gate, their voices rising above the din, hard and arrogant, shouting at each other and to the starter. All of them had supreme confidence in their ability to wring every last ounce of speed out of their mounts by the use of massive wrists and broad, thick hands. Slim, all muscle and bone, they sat on their racing machines and waited.

The bell clanged and the stall doors flew open! Instinctively, Alec let

The bell clanged and the stall doors flew open!
Instinctively, Alec let the reins slide through his hands.

the reins slide through his hands, his voice joining the cries of the other riders, "Yah! Yah! Yah!"

His hands suddenly tightened on the reins again, squeezing rather than pulling, as a horse moved directly in front of them and stayed there. Alec looked for racing room, knowing he'd been caught unprepared. He tried every trick he knew to get the Black free of the rush of bodies on every side of him.

His whip came down, not touching the Black, in an attempt to scare off the packed horses and riders. The wind carried his shouts to the other jockeys, his words threatening and challenging, those of a rider fighting for racing room and, perhaps, his very life. He drove his heels into the Black's sides and his hands went forward in brutal suddenness, urging the horse forward with all his strength.

They raced down the long backstretch chute.

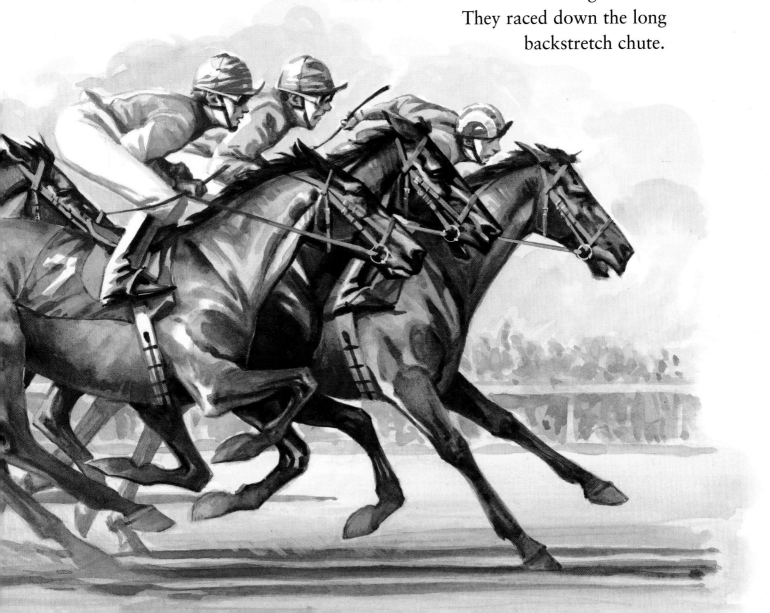

There were three furlongs to go to the far turn, two furlongs around the bend, and two more furlongs for home. He had to get the Black free and running before they reached the turn, for the stallion's long strides made it difficult to negotiate turns and he was apt to run out, losing ground. There might not be enough distance left in the stretch run to overtake the leaders.

Alec looked for a clear way through the traffic jam. He let the Black out another notch, not truly knowing where he was going anyway, for his need to do something was very great. He felt not only anger with himself but guilt. He sought relief in speed and more speed, and danger as well.

He had made a mistake, but there was time to correct it. He leaned into the Black, taking him over to the rail, only to pull him up abruptly when the opening he had spotted was closed by a plunging horse. Alec took the stallion back, moving towards the middle of the pack, inches away from the heaving hindquarters of horses directly ahead.

The Black was fighting for his head, trying to run over the horses in front of him.

The Black was fighting for his head, trying to run over the horses in front of him. Beyond the bunched field, two horses were free and clear. Light-weighted sprinters, their legs moved in short, piston-like strides, taking them towards the far turn like small, wound up whirlwinds. Alec knew he had to get after them soon or the Black would be beaten.

He tried to move the stallion between two outside horses but was shut off again. He had to bring the Black almost to a stop to avoid going down; his hands took a tight hold on the reins and he jerked hard. The force of it wrenched the bit in the stallion's mouth, tearing the flesh at the corners.

He heard the Black scream in rage and pain, and his heart felt a deep anguish. Yet he'd no alternative if he wanted to avoid serious injury ... even death. Suddenly he saw an opening and launched the Black forwards again.

Lathered foam whipped from the stallion's neck as he shot between horses. None of the jockeys had expected such a rush from behind with so little room between them. Above the din of racing hoofs, Alec heard the challenges the other riders hurled at him. One false step and the Black would go down. He guided him through the mass of horseflesh in a single rush, avoiding hoofs and bodies by inches. He rode as he never had before, using all his wits and skill with a strength and harshness he had not known he possessed. His daring, combined with the Black's fury and speed astonished the others and threw them off balance. They separated, and the leaping black stallion sped between them, free and clear!

Leaving the pack behind, Alec took the Black into the turn with only the two front-running sprinters ahead. They were setting a dizzy pace. Had he still the time and distance to catch them? The Black devoured the track with his long strides, yet ran wide going around the turn. Alec tried to guide him over to the rail but his extreme speed made it impossible. The leaders were already leaving the turn and entering the home stretch with just two furlongs to go.

Alec flattened himself against the stallion's neck, his face buried in the mane. There was no need to urge the Black on, for the racing stallion knew what was expected of him. He came off the turn, stretched low to the ground in the fury of his run. He was catching the leaders fast, outrunning them with every magnificent stride.

The crowd was on its feet. Was this to be the day the Black lost for the first time? The two leaders flashed by the sixteenth pole, their strides coming as one, a closely matched team of two, fighting, clawing their way to the finish wire.

The Black came down the track with a swiftness that could not be denied. But the fans were not really aware of the awesome power of his body, for he ran with such ease that his strides seemed to be a single flowing movement.

The finish wire was far enough away for Alec to know that the distance had not run out on them. He shouted into the wind created by his horse. Only the Black heard his cry of victory, but he was the only one that mattered. He caught the leaders two strides from the wire and swept under it all by himself.

... he ran with such ease that his strides seemed to be a single flowing movement.

FLAT RACING

The Black is a champion flat-racing horse. This form of racing, where horses race on a course without jumps, is the fastest type of race. As described in the story, the sport is full of excitement and tension both for the horses and jockeys taking part, and the huge number of spectators who pack the stands.

Royal patron
Racing is known as "the sport of kings" because of its long association with the British monarchy. King Henry VIII was the first royal patron of horse racing.

Alec and the Black's race is a short distance of 7/8ths of a mile. Most flat races are over a mile long. Horses may reach speeds of 65 kms an hour (40 miles per hour).

Thoroughbred
Thoroughbred horses are used in all forms of horse-racing. They have been bred over the last 200 years for their speed, courage, strength and stamina.

Weighty matters
Champion racehorses, like the Black, carry lead weights in the saddle added to the weight of the jockey as a handicap. The combined weight of the jockey and saddle is checked before and after a race.

Flat out
British jockeys take their racehorses out for early morning training gallops every day of the year whatever the weather. They train hard for the 16 national flat races held in the UK between March and October.

MY FRIEND FLICKA

from the novel by Mary O'Hara

Flicka, an unbroken, part-mustang filly, belongs to a boy named Ken who lives on a ranch in Wyoming USA. She is ill with fever, brought on by infected wounds, and rapidly wasting away. Ken's father believes Flicka is sure to die. He wants Gus, one of his ranch hands, to put her out of her misery, but Ken is determined to cure his beloved pony.

After supper, Ken carried Flicka her oats, but she would hardly touch them. She stood with her head hanging, but when he stroked it and talked to her, she pressed her face into his chest and was content.

He could feel the burning heat of her body. It didn't seem possible that anything so thin could be alive.

Presently Ken saw Gus coming into the pasture carrying the Winchester. When he saw Ken, he changed his direction and sauntered along as if he was out to shoot cottontails.

Ken ran to him, "When are you going to do it, Gus?"

"Ay was goin' down soon now, before it got dark –"

"Gus, don't do it tonight. Wait till morning. Just one more night, Gus."

"Vell, in de morning den, but it got to be done, Ken. Yer fadder gives de order."

"I know. I won't say anything more."

Gus went back to the bunk house and Ken returned to Flicka.

He stood by her, smoothing and caressing her as he always did. Usually he talked to her, but he couldn't do that now. There was only one thing in his mind, and he couldn't talk about that. Now and then, as if it came from someone else, he heard a little moan. It was he himself that was moaning.

Below the cottonwood trees, the darkness fell swiftly, and Ken and Flicka were hidden in it together. It folded them around and held them close. He couldn't see her, and she couldn't see him, but he moved around her, and her head turned to follow him so that her muzzle rested against him, as she always did. The darkness pressed them closer together.

At nine o'clock Howard [a ranch hand] was sent by Nell [Ken's mother] to call Ken. He stood at the corral gate, shouting.

Again there was the sound of soft moaning. Then Ken pressed a last kiss

"Gus, don't do it tonight. Wait till morning. Just one more night, Gus."

75

on Flicka's face, and went up the hill under the cottonwoods.

Flicka was still standing in her nursery when the full moon rose at ten. It was the Hunter's Moon, as yellow as the Harvest Moon, but not so large.

The night was silent, with the profound silence of a sea becalmed. Even the faint roaring of the earth, like the roaring in a shell, was hushed. It waited.

If the mind of a living being – man or beast – is clear, there are forewarnings of the approach of death. The body gets ready. One by one the active functions cease, till, at last, the currents of living force become inverted in a down-whirling spiral into which the creature is drawn, spinning faster and faster towards the vortex.

Though, from force of habit, she stood by the feed box, she had not touched the oats.

All of this can be felt; and, feeling this, Flicka knew that her time had come.

Her head hung low. Her legs were slightly splayed under her. Though, from force of habit, she stood by the feed box, she had not touched the oats. Every cell in her body was seared with fierce, burning fever, and sometimes her mind was in a drifting delirium, sometimes in coma, sometimes clear and knowing.

Flicka's wounds did not pain her, but the suction of the down-whirling spiral was an agony felt through every part of her. Now and then her young body found strength to fight against it; she struggled; she lifted her head. She turned towards the path down which Ken's running feet had come a thousand times that summer. He was all she had, and all she could hope for; but tonight, there was no sound, no step, no help.

For minutes she stayed so, her ears strained for the sound of him, longing and listening, then gradually succumbed to the tug of those inner quicksands, and drooped, wavering, over the earth.

In one of the surges of rebellion, she neighed.

Miles away on the upland, her sire, Banner, heard and answered. And the loud kingly cry, made into a faint trumpet call by the distance, drifted across the miles, across the roads, across the barbed wire barricades that intervened, and burned a cross-fire of hope into the fever that was consuming Flicka,

She began to prance jerkily, like a marionette pulled by strings. All that was left in her of will and power gathered itself and she trotted downstream along the bank.

She jarred to a sudden stop, standing in terror with head low and feet braced out as if she had come face to face with a phantom. Gradually the terror went out of her, but she held the ridiculous posture as if unable to move. Her head turned again to the ranch house ... *would he come?*

She was thirsty. The smell of the fresh running water drew her. She waded into the stream and drank, got her fill, lifted her head, turned it again to the house. The cool water rippled against her legs.

There was no sound from the house, no feet running upon the path, and suddenly the last of her strength was gone. Lunging forward, she fell, half on the bank, half in the water, and lay there, struggling convulsively.

At last she was still.

Some minutes later, from ten miles away on the towering black-timbered shoulders of Pole Mountain, there stole out the most desolate cry in all the world – the howl of the grey timber wolf. It rode on the upper air without a tremor, high and thin, pointed as a needle.

Ken had seen the Hunter's Moon rise over the eastern horizon before he went upstairs. He hadn't completely undressed, but he had the sheet drawn up to his chin, in case his mother or father came in to look at him. He heard them talking together in their room as they undressed.

She was thirsty. The smell of the fresh running water drew her.

How long they took. It seemed to him hours before the whole house was quiet – as quiet as the night was outside.

He heard Flicka neigh, but he didn't hear Banner answer. Human ears were not keen enough to catch that distant greeting. He knew Flicka was neighing for him. He heard the wolf howl.

He waited another hour, till everyone was so deep asleep there would be no chance of their hearing. Then he stole out of bed and put on the rest of his clothes.

He carried his shoes and crept down the hall, past the door of his parents' room, taking half a minute a step.

On the far end of the terrace, he sat down and put on his shoes, his heart pounding and the blood almost suffocating him.

He kept whispering, "I'm coming, Flicka – I'm coming – "

His feet pattered down the path. He ran as fast as he could.

It was so dark under the cottonwood trees, he had to stand a moment, getting used to the darkness, before he could be sure that Flicka was not there. There stood her feed box – but the filly was gone.

He ran wildly here and there. At last, when there was no sign of her, he began a systematic search all through the pasture. He dared not call aloud, but he whispered – "Flicka – oh, Flicka – where are you?"

At last he found her down the creek lying in the water. Her head had been on the bank, but as she lay there, the current of the stream had sucked and pulled at her, and she had had no strength to resist; and little by little her head had slipped down until, when Ken got there, only the muzzle was resting on the bank, and the body and legs were swinging in the stream.

Ken slid into the water, sitting on the bank, and he hauled at her head. But she was heavy, and the current dragged like a weight; and he began to sob because he had no strength to draw her out.

Then he found a leverage for his heels against some rocks in the bed of the stream, and he braced himself against them, and pulled with all his might; and her head came up on to his knees, and he held it cradled in his arms.

He was glad she had died of her own accord, in the cool water, under the moon, instead of being shot by Gus. Then, putting his face close to hers, and looking searchingly into her eyes, he saw that she was alive and looking back at him.

The long night passed.

The moon slowly slid across the heavens.

The water rippled over Ken's legs, and over Flicka's body. And gradually the heat and the fever went out of her, and the cool running water washed and washed her wounds.

That night took a heavy toll from Ken, but for Flicka there was resurgence. At the moment when Ken drew her into his arms and cried her name, the spring of the down-whirling spiral was broken, Flicka was released and not once again did she feel it.

Ken slid into the water, sitting on the bank, and he hauled at her head. But she was heavy, and the current dragged like a weight.

The life-currents in her body turned, and in weak and wavering fashion, flowed upwards. A power went into her from Ken; all his youth and strength and magnetism given her freely and abundantly on the stream of his love – from his ardent eyes to hers.

But for Ken, there was, first, the creeping numbness of those parts where the head and neck of the filly pressed. Then the deep chill from the cold water running over his legs, his thighs, almost up to his waist. Long before the night was over, his teeth were chattering and his body shaking with chills.

It didn't matter. Nothing mattered but that he should hold Flicka, and hold the life in her.

At the moment when Ken drew her into his arms and cried her name, the spring of the down-whirling spiral was broken; Flicka was released and not once again did she feel it.

BASIC HORSE CARE

The horse is the biggest and most easily injured of all the domesticated animals. Looking after one and making sure it stays healthy takes up a lot of time and is a big responsibility. But with the right care, good exercise, and proper feeding you will have a loyal and trusty animal who may live to be over 30 years old.

Mucking out
A healthy horse must have a clean and tidy stable. All the droppings and dirty straw must be removed every day.

A horse that is unwell should be kept in a stable for box rest and not ridden.

Regular exercise
To keep fit, horses kept in a stable should be taken out for exercise at least two hours a day. If you don't have time to ride your horse, it can be exercised on a lungeing rein for 20 minutes instead.

Balanced diet
Feeding your horse a good diet will help keep it healthy. Horses have small stomachs so they need to eat small amounts often. Hay and fresh drinking water provide enough basic nutrition. Ready-mixed cereals provide extra vitamins and minerals.

ANTISEPTIC LIQUID

COLD TREATMENT PACK

BANDAGE

SCISSORS

First aid kit
A basic first aid kit is essential to treat any minor injuries or wounds. A vet should be called to treat any serious illness or injury.

JILL'S GYMKHANA

from the novel by Ruby Ferguson

Jill has always dreamed of having her own pony. After overcoming many trials and tribulations, she manages to buy Danny Boy, learn to ride, and enter Chatton Show. This extract comes from the first in a highly popular series of novels.

"What lovely jumps," said Ann.

"They look like precipices to me," I remarked. "But they are lovely, just the same."

We were leaning over the railings to watch the first event after the interval which was the Open Jumping. I always think this event is the most wonderful thing in the world to watch; there is something utterly splendid about it, to see the tall magnificent horses soar into the air under their skilful riders' touch, all in such harmony and effortless control. Everything around is beautiful, too; the white painted jumps and the bright green field, the eager faces round the ring and the grandstand packed with people ready to cheer. And to think that there are actually people who never go to gymkhanas! It makes me think of those noble lines of the poet,

"Breathes there the man with soul so dead,

Who never to himself hath said,

'I will arise and go to a gymkhana?'"

When number thirty-three was called we saw Mrs Darcy ride into the ring on a lovely lean grey called Martha, who I knew from my own experience was capable of anything if she could keep her temperament in control. This was one of Martha's good days, and she jumped a beautifully collected round, finishing with only one and a half faults.

"I think she's got a chance," I said excitedly.

However, a strange man on a black hunter won first place with no faults, and a boy of twenty who we were told had won Firsts all over the country was second with one fault. To my joy, Mrs Darcy got third place, which was pretty good considering the competition, as there were nineteen entries.

The open event over, the stewards began to lower the jumps for the novice jumping. In this event I had the thrill of seeing my friend Angela jump a clear round on Inez, and everybody cheered like mad. In the end she tied for first place with a hunting man called Markham, who kept a lot of horses, and they jumped it off and Angela won! It was a great

We were leaning over the railings to
watch the first event after the interval
which was the Open Jumping.

Ann and I rode round to the collecting ring, and we both had the feeling that our hearts were jumping about inside and doing gymkhanas on their own.

honour to have won a First in the novice-jumping at Chatton Show.

Then the jumps were lowered again and this time it was US. So Ann and I rode round to the collecting ring, and we both had the feeling that our hearts were jumping about inside and doing gymkhanas on their own. In any case they say that if you don't have this feeling you are not much good.

There were twenty-six children competing, of all ages from twelve to sixteen; and there was the famous Maureen Chase looking cool and distant, and the famous Frank Stabley who I thought looked an awfully nice boy, and Susan Pyke, backing her pink horse into the others and getting black looks from everybody.

She kept saying, "I can't help it. He's so full of spirit. You see – he's a show jumper, not just an ordinary pony," – and she gave all our "ordinary" ponies very scornful glances.

"Well, you're in," said Ann to Susan, as a boy called Peters came riding back to the ring and the megaphone called out "Thirteen faults". "So you can let your charger charge!"

All eyes were on Susan as she made a spectacular entrance; but I didn't like the way the roan pawed the ground, or the look in his eye. He had a silly, wild look, not the sensible clever look of a pony who is going to do any good at jumping.

He went straight at the first jump, which was the bush, before Susan was ready, and nearly unseated her; however he cleared the jump with inches to spare, and a girl next to me said, "Some show jumper!"

Susan was now trying to collect her pony, but he refused to be collected. He went full tilt at the next jump, which was the gate, soared into the air, bucked in mid-air, got his feet in a knot, and sent Susan flying six yards. She landed with a thud, and the pink horse, having done his stuff, ran right out of the ring, neighing at the top of his voice.

Susan sat there on the ground, quite openly weeping for all to see. Two stewards went and helped her up, and there was obviously nothing the matter with her, so presently she landed back among us looking very low indeed.

"Serves her jolly well right!" said a girl next to me. "She always ruins every gymkhana for everybody else. They ought to disqualify her permanently."

Susan could not help hearing this remark, and Ann who was soft-hearted went across to her and said kindly, "It was jolly hard luck, Susan."

Susan sat there on the ground, quite openly weeping for all to see.

"Oh, thank you, Ann," said Susan, in a very humble and heartfelt tone, quite different from her usual bragging one.

Meanwhile Maureen Chase had gone in and done an efficient but uninspiring round, to finish up with two faults, and a boy called Michael Grant was making the crowd roar by sending everything flying.

Then it was Ann's turn, and I knew she would enjoy herself because she didn't expect much from Seraphine. To my surprise – and hers – Seraphine jumped the round of her life, finishing with only four faults, and she and Ann looked so pretty and graceful jumping that the crowd clapped and cheered like mad, and the judges all smiled with pleasure at Ann as she rode so neatly and nicely off.

Frank Stabley had very bad luck. He took four jumps perfectly, but just as he approached the triple bar, a dog fight broke out in the crowd only about five yards away. Frank's pony reared, and then being quite upset gave him three refusals. I was awfully sorry about this as Frank certainly was an excellent jumper.

Then my number was called. As I rode into the ring I had the strangest feeling of being most awfully happy, and I could tell that Danny Boy was feeling the same way. I whispered into his ear, "Now angel, don't bother about all those people. We're just jumping for fun, like we do at home, and it's going to be heavenly."

He arched his neck, and looked both proud and serious, and so at a collected canter we approached the first jump. I only had to whisper, "Hup!" and the next minute we were over, so smoothly that I had hardly felt him ride. I knew then that he was going to do it! I knew that he and I were just like one single person. So we took the gate, and then the wall, and then – with only the slightest pause – the tricky in-and-out. We were coming up to the triple bar now. I stroked his neck and whispered, "Don't rush, boy. Do just as I tell you." I had forgotten the crowd and everything except those three white bars ahead, sparkling in the sunshine. "Now!" I said suddenly. "Hup!"

And then I did feel him soar. I felt him gather his legs up in that lovely careful way of his, and I felt the rush of the wind on my face, and then I could hardly believe it for we were on the ground again and everybody was clapping and I wasn't quite conscious as I patted him and couldn't say a word as he carried me out of the ring and the megaphones blared, "Clear round".

And then I did feel him soar. I felt him gather his legs up in that lovely careful way of his.

87

Was this really me, or was I dreaming? Surely jumping a clear round in the under-sixteens at Chatton Show was the sort of thing that could only happen in a dream? But I came round when some of my friends began to thump me on the back until my tie nearly flew off, and I gasped, "Well, it's nothing really. About six other people are sure to jump clear rounds."

But strangely enough nobody else did, and presently three of us were called in. I was first, a boy called Lloyd was second with one fault, and Maureen Chase was third with two. After I had received my red rosette I was told that I must also go up to the grandstand to receive the Hopley Challenge Cup, to be held for a year. So with a scarlet face and hands that felt like hams I took this large silver cup in my arms, and muttered something like "Oh, thanks!" to somebody who I afterwards found out was Lord Hopley. And then my at-no-times-particularly-graceful exit was completely ruined when I dropped the black ebony base of the thing, which fell on the ground with a resounding thud and had to be rescued by a steward, while resounding howls of derision mingled with the cheers of the populace.

One place where I simply dare not look was the front row of the stand where Mummy and my own friends were sitting. I let myself go in the usual wild gallop round the ring; and when I came to the exit, there they all were.

"Good kid," was all that Martin said. And Mummy added, "Not bad at all, Jill, but why on earth did you have to drop that thing?"

"There's nothing left now but the Grand parade," said Martin. "Hand Danny Boy over to Bob here, who'll give him a rub down and you scoot off and have a wash and brush-up."

"OK," I said. "I'll want your powder, Mummy."

So with my cap, boots and jodhpurs brushed, my tie retied, and my face sophisticatedly powdered, I rejoined Danny Boy, who under Bob's skilful hand looked as if he was made of patent leather. Then headed by the local band we joined in the Grand parade – in which everything that has won Firsts in the Show marches slowly round and round the ring –

and Danny Boy gave me quite a look when he found he had to do a collected walk behind a lot of fat cows and dairy turn-outs.

At last it was all over. As I rode out I passed Frank Stabley and his father, and they smiled at me and heard Frank say, "Look, Dad, that's the girl who won. Pretty good, what?"

And Mr Stabley said, "They say that Martin Lowe trained her, so you'd expect something."

After I had received my red rosette I was told that I must also go up to the grandstand to receive the Hopley Challenge Cup, to be held for a year.

I was frightfully happy, but I didn't feel the least bit cocky or conceited, because I knew that I'd had a lot of luck and that this was the sort of day which only comes to a person once in a lifetime.

As we all left the showground together, there stood Mrs Darcy and gave me a gay salute.

"Well, well well!" she said, in her loud, hearty way. "It certainly has been Jill's gymkhana!"

And with those magic words ringing in my ears, I turned my pony happily towards home.

SHOW TIME!

Jill takes part in a show-jumping class, but there are also dressage, showing classes, and gymkhana games among the events at horse shows. However big or small the show, a lot of hard work is needed both before and on the day itself. But whether you win a prize or not, a show is sure to provide a fun and exciting day out for you and your pony.

Grooming
Careful grooming is needed before a show to make a pony's coat, mane , and tail shine and look as beautiful as possible on the day.

Getting to the show
If a pony needs to be transported to a show in a horsebox, it is important to arrive in plenty of time. A pony will need time to get used to his new surroundings.

Show jumping
Jill wins her show-jumping event because Danny Boy gets a clear round – he jumps over the course of fences without knocking any of the poles off.

Gymkhana games
As well as being fun, gymkhana games test a rider's balance and skill. Here, the rider has to lean over to pick up a bottle before racing back to the start of the course. The winner is the one who completes the task in the fastest time.

Prize winner
Jill describes what a wonderful feeling it is to win a prize. But it's a team effort and it's important to thank a pony, too.

THE FIRST MAN ON MANCHA'S BACK

from *The Tale of Two Horses* by A. F. Tschiffely

In the 1930s, A. F. Tschiffely made an epic two-and-a-half-year journey from the Argentine to Washington in the United States on his wild Criollo horses, Gato and Mancha. Here is Mancha's account of his breaking-in cowboy fashion, a quick and frightening experience.

One morning several cowboys came towards the corral, and as we nervously watched, we noticed that our master was among them.

Before I realized what all these men had come for, I was lassoed and pulled out of the corral. My legs were then tied in such a way that it was impossible for me to move or kick without falling. I was so frightened that I wasn't aware that a man strapped one of those strange things, called saddles, on my back. Almost at the same instant the ropes with which my legs were bound were untied and taken off.

At first I thought the thing on my back was a puma or some other wild animal, so I arched my back and put my head between my fore-legs, and bucked for all I was worth. I fought with terror and fury and tried every trick I knew to throw enemies off my back.

Only wild horses know how to buck properly, for if an enemy leaps on them they must do this to shake him off, and thus save their lives. Pumas and tigers usually jump on their victims' backs and bite their necks to kill them. To throw them off, we put our heads between our fore-legs and arch our backs – like cats do when they see a dog – and then we buck as hard as we can.

I fought so furiously that I raised a cloud of dust, but every time

I bucked I heard a loud "hee-hoo!" Soon I found out that it was not a puma, but a cowboy who was sitting on my back, and I noticed that the other men were looking on and waving their hats. Realising that I simply couldn't shake off the man by bucking, I thought I'd try to flee; so I madly raced over the prairie.

I arched my back and put my head between my fore-legs, and bucked for all I was worth.

Every now and then I stopped suddenly, but even this didn't move the man whose whip and spurs urged me on, faster and faster.

Seeing a tree, I decided to race towards it, and there brush off the rider, but before I had gone far, two cowboys on horses came alongside me and pushed me in the other direction. After a while I was so tired and out of breath that I simply could run and buck no more, so I stood still, trembling all over. I had lost the fight. The gaucho was still on my back. What a man! How he could ride!

When I had been guided back to the corral, the saddle was taken off me and placed on Gato, whose resistance was also in vain.

Although I was dripping with perspiration, and shaking all over with exhaustion, I watched what was happening to my pal outside.

He fought so bravely that all our friends in the wilds would have been very proud of him, but again the man proved to be a good rider – and poor Gato also lost his fight. Puffing and panting and with flecks of foam all over him, he was brought back into the corral, and when the cowboys had gone, and we had cooled off a little, the two of us had a long talk about our latest experience with men.

For a few days after this we were saddled and ridden. We soon realized that our riders intended us no harm; and as it was no use struggling against them, we slowly gave in. Once or twice we managed to throw off the rider, but he always fell on his feet like a cat, and before we had time to run away he was on our backs again.

Very soon we gave up bucking, and, instead, trotted or cantered in whatever direction our riders guided us.

When we were not being ridden we were kept in the corral; and we began to wonder if we would ever be let out again to join our pals who were happily grazing outside in the big field.

Somehow we felt that something was to happen soon, and as the days passed we felt this more and more.

BRONCO BUSTING

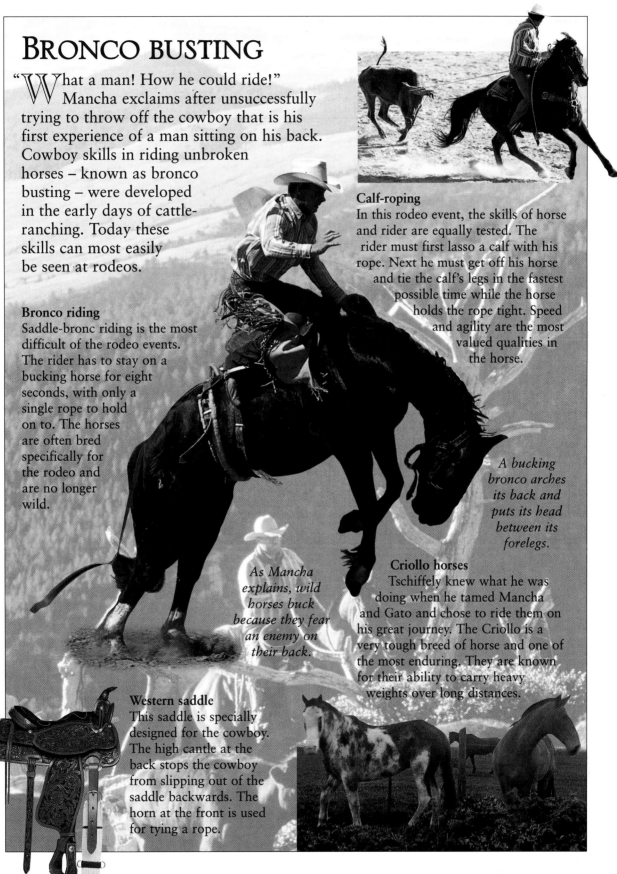

"What a man! How he could ride!" Mancha exclaims after unsuccessfully trying to throw off the cowboy that is his first experience of a man sitting on his back. Cowboy skills in riding unbroken horses – known as bronco busting – were developed in the early days of cattle-ranching. Today these skills can most easily be seen at rodeos.

Bronco riding
Saddle-bronc riding is the most difficult of the rodeo events. The rider has to stay on a bucking horse for eight seconds, with only a single rope to hold on to. The horses are often bred specifically for the rodeo and are no longer wild.

Calf-roping
In this rodeo event, the skills of horse and rider are equally tested. The rider must first lasso a calf with his rope. Next he must get off his horse and tie the calf's legs in the fastest possible time while the horse holds the rope tight. Speed and agility are the most valued qualities in the horse.

A bucking bronco arches its back and puts its head between its forelegs.

As Mancha explains, wild horses buck because they fear an enemy on their back.

Criollo horses
Tschiffely knew what he was doing when he tamed Mancha and Gato and chose to ride them on his great journey. The Criollo is a very tough breed of horse and one of the most enduring. They are known for their ability to carry heavy weights over long distances.

Western saddle
This saddle is specially designed for the cowboy. The high cantle at the back stops the cowboy from slipping out of the saddle backwards. The horn at the front is used for tying a rope.

ACKNOWLEDGMENTS

The publishers would like to thank the copyright holders for permission
to reproduce the following copyright material:
Monica Edwards: for "The Champions". Copyright © The Estate of Monica Edwards. Reprinted by
permission of Barlows on behalf of the Estate. **Walter Farley:** for the extract from *The Black Stallion
and the Girl.* Copyright © 1971 by Walter Farley. Reprinted by permission of Random House Inc.
Ruby Ferguson: for the extract from *Jill's Gymkhana,* published by Hodder and Stoughton Ltd.
Copyright © Ruby Ferguson 1949. Reproduced by permission of Hodder and Stoughton Ltd.
Marguerite Henry: for the extract from *Misty of Chincoteague.* Copyright © 1947 and copyright
renewed © 1975 Marguerite Henry. Reprinted with the permission of Simon & Schuster Books for
Young Readers, an imprint of Simon & Schuster Children's Publishing Division. **Roger Lancelyn Green:**
for "Pegasus", originally published by G. Bell & Sons Ltd as "The Prince and the Flying Horse", from
Old Greek Fairy Stories (1958). Copyright © Richard Lancelyn Green. Reprinted with permission of
the Literary Estate of Roger Lancelyn Green. **Elyne Mitchell:** for the extract from *The Silver Brumby,*
published by HarperCollins Australia. Copyright © Elyne Mitchell 1958. Reprinted by permission of
Curtis Brown (Aust) Pty Ltd., Sydney. **Mary O'Hara:** for the extract from *My Friend Flicka,* published
by Egmont Children's Books. Copyright © Mary O'Hara 1941. Reprinted by permission of Laurence
Pollinger Limited and the Estate of Mary O'Hara. **Diana Pullein-Thompson:** Jennifer Luithlen Agency
for an extract from *A Foal for Candy* by Diana Pullein-Thompson, published by Hutchinson.
Copyright © 1981 Diana Pullein-Thompson. **A.F. Tschiffely:** for the extract from *The Tale of Two
Horses.* John Johnson Ltd on behalf of the Estate. Copyright © The Estate of A. F. Tschiffely 1934.
Every effort has been made to obtain permission to reproduce copyright material but there
may be cases where we have been unable to trace a copyright holder. Dorling Kindersley
will be happy to correct any omissions in future printings.

Further photography by: Geoff Brightling, Peter Chadwick, Gordon Clayton,
Andy Crawford, Bob Langrish, Tim Ridley, Karl Shone, Jerry Young,

t = top, b = bottom, c = centre, l = left, r = right, a = above, bgr = background.

AKG London Ltd: 31bgr, tl; Art & Ancient Architecture: 31cr;
Bridgeman Art Library: 15tl, 31clb; Christie's Images: 63bgr;
Mary Evans Picture Library: 25tr, 47bgr, 63cl; Kit Houghton: 7tr,
25c, br, 47bl; Bob Langrish: 15bgr, 31bl, 41tl, 63bl, br, 73bgr, tr,
br, c, 91bgr, cl, c, 95c; Peter Newark's Americana: 95br; Frank
Spooner Pictures: 95bgr, tr; Tony Stone Images: 15bl; 25bgr, cl, bl.